"Are you a witch to be feared?"

She looked up and he felt the smoldering heat of her anger. "Are you like all the others, my lord? Eager to use my gifts when it suits your purpose, then resorting to cruel names to brand me different?"

He reached for his goblet, avoiding her eyes. Her words were too close to the mark, and shamed him. But he'd be damned if he'd ask forgiveness of this...this tart-tongued female.

"We waste time talking, woman. We'll eat, and then you can return your attention to my son."

Allegra shivered as cold settled into her bones. Whatever tenuous truce they'd attempted, it had dissolved like the wisps of fog that often drifted over the Enchanted Loch until banished by the sun.

The man across the table was once more the demanding lord. And she, like it or not, his unwilling captive.

* * *

Highland Sword
Harlequin Historical #654—April 2003

RUTH LANGAN

HIGHLAND SWORD

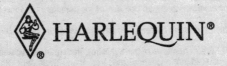

HARLEQUIN®

TORONTO • NEW YORK • LONDON
AMSTERDAM • PARIS • SYDNEY • HAMBURG
STOCKHOLM • ATHENS • TOKYO • MILAN • MADRID
PRAGUE • WARSAW • BUDAPEST • AUCKLAND

ISBN 0-373-29254-6

HIGHLAND SWORD

For Maureen,
who puts the bubbles in champagne to shame.

And of course for Tom.
Always.

Prologue

Scotland—1540

The pewter sky was boiling with clouds threatening rain. A chill wind ruffled the tall grass growing across the meadow. The weather didn't deter the populace from enjoying market day. Those on foot cast a wary eye on horse-drawn carts and hay wagons vying for space along the narrow roads leading to Edinburgh.

Nola Drummond, a young widow, threaded her pony cart through the crowd. Her mother, Wilona, was seated beside her. In the back were Nola's three little daughters, sitting atop the bundles of dried herbs, skeins of yarn and baskets of eggs, which the women sold at market. Crowded in beside them were Bessie, a withered old crone with a hunched back, and Jeremy, a fat little troll dressed in a tiny top hat and frock coat. Both Bessie and Jeremy had been shunned by others before being taken in by this family.

"Look, Mum." Six-year-old Allegra pointed to the crowd of people gathered around the banks of the loch.

When their little cart drew closer, they could see women and children weeping as they stood watching a group of fishermen hauling the body of a young lad from the water.

Nola reined in the pony, bringing their cart to a halt. She and Wilona, helped five-year-old Kylia and three-year-old Gwenellen to the ground before starting toward the others.

Unable to control her curiosity, Allegra was already out of the cart and running ahead. Once she'd reached the shore, it was an easy matter to inch her way through the crowd until she could see and hear everything.

"Nay! Not my Jamie." A woman threw herself upon the body of the lad, her voice hoarse from sobbing. "I've already buried my man, and three of my babes. Jamie is all I have left in this world. Oh, no. Please. Not my Jamie, too."

One of the fishermen laid a big hand on the woman's shoulder. "I'm sorry, Mary. But the lad is gone. We were too late to save him."

A wave of terrible sadness swept the bystanders.

Even the fishermen, hardened by years at sea, could no longer hold back their tears as the woman gave in to a fit of sobbing.

Caught up in the emotion of the crowd, Allegra crept forward until she was standing beside the distraught woman. Before anyone could stop her she knelt and placed her hands on the lad's chest.

At once she was seized with a violent tremor as the icy shock was absorbed into her fingertips and passed through her body. The water of the loch had been cold. So very cold.

Shivering, Allegra looked up at his mother. "Your Jamie isn't dead."

"What are you saying?" Caught between surprise at the child's boldness and a need to believe, the woman narrowed her eyes on her.

"He isn't dead. He wants to come back to you, but he needs help."

With jaws slack, the crowd watched in horrified fascination as this wee stranger pressed her palms hard against his chest.

Water spilled out of the lad's mouth. His mother let out a scream, but Allegra didn't seem to hear. She was like one in a trance, her gaze fixed on him with such intensity, her green eyes seemed to burn with an inner fire.

It was a shocking image. This tiny lass, like some wild creature, fiery hair falling in tangles to below her waist, ignoring the cries of the crowd as she began to speak to the lad in an ancient tongue that even the oldest among them had forgotten.

When the words ended she bent low, pressing her mouth on his.

Suddenly his body began to twitch.

"What trickery is this?" someone shouted. "Take the lass in hand and spare this poor mother."

But before the crowd could react, the lad's body gave a violent shudder and his eyes opened.

"Oh, Jamie! Sweet heaven." His mother let out a cry, sweeping him into her arms and crushing him against her chest. "It's my Jamie. Back from the dead."

As the crowd surged forward, Nola pushed her way through and caught her daughter by the arm, hauling her roughly aside. "Get into the cart now, Allegra." Nola's eyes darted with nervousness. "Hurry now, child."

Up ahead, Allegra could see her grandmother already bundling Kylia and Gwenellen into the back of the cart, where she hurriedly covered them with furs.

As soon as Allegra and her mother climbed up to the seat of the cart, Wilona flicked the reins and the horse took off at a run.

Allegra glanced from her mother to her grandmother, who wore matching looks of fear. "Did I do something wrong?"

"Nay, child. But there were many watching. You've been warned that we're not like others."

The little girl hung her head. "I'm sorry. But Jamie's mother was crying. And in my head I could hear him crying, too. He wanted to come back to her. He said as much."

Nola gathered her daughter close and hugged her. "You did nothing wrong, Allegra. But there are some who don't understand our gifts."

"Why?"

"Because they've forgotten the ancient ways. They've turned away from the healing powers within their hearts."

The little girl looked solemn as she folded her hands in her lap. "I'm glad we haven't turned away from the power." She closed her eyes and leaned against her mother, giving in to the weakness that laid claim to her.

Nola sighed and glanced over her daughter's head to meet her own mother's shadowed gaze. "I hope you'll never have cause to regret it, Allegra."

The midnight moon was obscured by heavy clouds that swirled in an angry sky. A lone rider clattered over the cobblestones of the courtyard. The sound of his approach had the hounds leaping at the barred door.

Wilona slipped out of bed and hushed the animals before throwing the latch and peering into the darkness. Her unbound hair, laced with gray, spilled around a face stiff with concern.

Recognizing the man as a distant cousin, she opened the door wider and stood aside. "What brings you here at such an hour, Duncan?"

"There's talk at the tavern, Wilona." He fidgeted with discomfort, unable to meet her eyes.

His gaze skimmed over the troll asleep by the fire. The creature was rumored to have slept under a bridge until rescued by these good women. At a footfall on the stair he looked over and saw Bessie, the old crone who was thought to be a seer. She, too, had been an outcast until she found refuge in this place.

"You risk too much by allowing the lasses to display their gifts to the world."

"Allegra has always had a tender heart. We couldn't stop her. Would you rather she'd let the lad die, Duncan?"

The man flushed. "I don't pretend to understand how you and yours come to possess such powers. Nor do I hold with those who say it's the mark of the devil. But I fear for you, Wilona. You go too far when you take in misfits and otherwordly creatures." he nodded toward Bessie, who eyed him in silence.

"She was turned out by her people. She had nowhere to go."

He sighed. "These are troubling times. You know that music, dancing and all manner of frivolity are the devil's own works. There are those who intend to go to Edinburgh on the morrow to report this unholy deed. You and yours could be sent to Tolbooth Prison, or worse, the lot of you could be put to death."

"What would you have us do, Duncan? Become like others, cruel and uncaring? Turn our backs on our precious gifts? Gifts that can benefit others? You well know that we've never used our gifts for our own profit."

He gave a bleak shake of his head and started toward the door. As he pulled it open and stepped out into the night he paused. "This visit never happened. You never heard from me. If pressed, I'll admit that we are distantly related, as are all from the ancient clan Drummond. But I'll not subject my wife and children to the anger of a mob thirsty for blood."

Wilona nodded. "I understand, Duncan. And I'm sorry for whatever trouble this brings upon your head."

After bolting the door she turned to see her daughter standing in the shadows. "You heard?"

Nola nodded. "Aye."

"We feared this day would come." The older woman's spine stiffened. "For the sake of the lasses, we must return to the Mystical Kingdom, and we must leave now, so that there is no trace of us on the morrow."

"But the isolation? It was the reason we left."

At Nola's words the older woman held up a hand to silence her. "Indeed. But isolation if preferable to the dangers we face here."

"What of Bessie and Jeremy?" Nola watched as the troll sat up and rubbed sleep from his eyes.

"They are welcome to come with us if they choose. Bessie?"

The old woman nodded.

"Jeremy?"

The little troll got to his feet and began to pull on his frock coat.

While Bessie and Jeremy prepared the cart for a journey to the Highlands, Nola and Wilona carried the sleeping children to a nest of furs in the back. As silent as a summer breeze they set off, with the hounds running alongside.

Before the morning sun had risen, the cottage lay empty. The mother, daughter and three granddaughters, as well as a troll and a hunchbacked crone, had left without a trace.

Some said it was a certain sign that they'd aligned themselves with the devil, and had descended into darkness. Others spoke in whispers about a land in the Highlands that had long been home to their clan. An enchanted land, where those with special gifts would be free to practice their mystical powers, away from the prying eyes of disbelievers.

Chapter One

Mystical Kingdom—1559

"Allegra, you've worked long enough." Kylia wiped a strand of coal-black hair from her cheek and paused beside the garden row where her sister was busy hoeing. "Now come fishing with me."

"How I'd love to. But I've another row to see to."

"It will keep. And you'll feel so fresh and cool when you splash barefoot in the stream with me."

"Aye. I'd like that." Allegra mopped at the sweat that beaded her brow. "As soon as I finish here, I'll join you."

"Promise?"

"I do."

Kylia smiled, for the pleasure was always greater when shared with her sister. As she swung away, her youngest sister, Gwenellen, came racing across the meadow, followed by Jeremy. Though he'd once been known as a fierce troll, exacting payment from all who crossed his bridge, Jeremy had found contentment here in the Mystical Kingdom.

"Allegra. Jeremy and I have found a marvelous berry patch in the forest."

The little troll nodded. "They're the sweetest yet." His voice resembled that of a frog croaking. "Come with us and help us pick them, Allegra."

She shook her head. "First I have to finish my chore. Then I promised Kylia I'd fish with her. But if you two are still in the forest when I've finished with all that, I'll help."

Gwenellen shot her sister a pixie smile. "Here. Let me finish your chore right now." Before Allegra could stop her she clapped her hands and chanted, "Be gone, weeds. Do as I wish."

Almost at once a shower of seeds fell from the sky, followed by a net filled with fish.

Gwenellen looked around in dismay, then lifted her head to shout, "Not seeds. Weeds. And I didn't say fish, I said wish."

Allegra was convulsed with laughter. "Oh, Gwenellen. You really need to practice your spells."

"I suppose I do." Her younger sister's frown turned into a smile. "Well, it looks like you'll have to weed your garden after all. But when you're done, promise you'll join us?''

"If you're still in the forest picking berries.''

Gwenellen nodded. "We'll probably still be there. You know we always eat one for every one we drop in my basket.''

Allegra laughed as she glanced at Jeremy patting his round tummy. "I know. Just try not to eat so many that you can't make it back in time to sup.''

"Have you ever known me to be late for supper?'' With her laughter ringing on the air, the fair-haired lass danced off to the forest in search of her berries, with the little troll racing to keep up.

Just then Allegra's grandmother, Wilona, made her way along the neat rows of the garden, and paused beside her granddaughter, bent to her hoeing. "You're doing a fine job, Allegra.''

The lass paused to wipe her forehead with the back of her hand. "I enjoy watching the tender shoots breaking through the ground, Gram. The birth of each small plant is such a wondrous thing.''

"Aye.'' Wilona smiled at this. It was so typical of her eldest granddaughter. Despite her practical nature, Allegra had the most tender of hearts. She could do the work of three people, then take on another chore, just to give her sisters a chance to swim or bask in the early-summer sun.

The older woman glanced around. "Where are your sisters?"

"Kylia is down by the stream, no doubt already splashing like a fish."

The old woman shared a smile with her. "Aye. That one does love the water. Let's just hope she remembers to fetch some of those fish for our supper. And Gwenellen?"

"Off in the forest with Jeremy, hunting berries." Allegra wisely refrained from mentioning the latest failed spell, for their grandmother had despaired of ever teaching her youngest granddaughter the skills the others enjoyed with such ease.

"The lass does have a fondness for sweets. As does Jeremy." Wilona frowned. "Still, it isn't fair to leave you with the garden chores while they're off playing."

"I don't mind, Gram." Allegra scraped at the earth, dislodging a patch of weeds. "There's nowhere I'd rather be than right here. This is as pleasant to me as the water is to Kylia, and the soothing forest to Gwenellen."

"I understand, for it was always the same with me." The older woman filled her pockets with greens before turning away. "But you've already mucked the stalls and collected bundles of herbs for your mother's potions."

Allegra smiled at the mention of Bessie. Her gifts

were many, including the ability to sing like an angel. Allegra and her sisters had learned a score of lullabyes from the old woman, who'd often sung them to sleep in their young days.

"When you finish here, come back to the cottage and help yourself to the stew Bessie and I have simmering."

"I will, Gram." Allegra kissed her grandmother's cheek before returning to her work.

She had chosen this spot for the garden because it lay in a high meadow, surrounded by forest on either side. Here in the sunlight, under her watchful care, fat cabbages grew to the size of a man's head. Neat rows of kale and chard grew alongside sage and thyme.

It wasn't an easy task to keep the wild things from taking over the garden plot. It took diligence on Allegra's part. She devoted several hours each day during the short summer months to tilling the soil and attacking the weeds that threatened. Her mother and grandmother had taught her how to build a wattle fence of green willow branches and twigs, intricately woven to keep the forest creatures at bay.

Around her, the meadow was a sea of heather, the graceful purple blossoms swaying in the gentle breeze. Out of nowhere a shadow fell over her. Puzzled, she glanced heavenward. A hawk, perhaps. Or a thundercloud. The sky was sunny and clear, without a single cloud to mar its beauty. There was no sign of a bird. Alarmed, she looked around to see what had caused the shadow.

Too late, she saw the figure of a blood-spattered giant, mouth set in a tight line, eyes narrowed on her with grim concentration. In his hands was a length of plaid that he tossed over her, pinning her arms to her sides, covering her head to blot out the light and still her cries.

She struggled, and managed to kick her legs until even they were wrapped firmly. Swaddled as helplessly as an infant, she was unable to move.

She could hear the sound of his breathing as he raced through the meadow, carrying her slung over his shoulder. Once in the forest he paused to pull himself into the saddle while holding her firmly in his arms. Then the horse was running, the wind rushing past them as he urged his steed ever faster. Tree branches slapped and snagged, and she could hear the giant's occasional muttered curse. But though they splashed through streams and clattered over rocks, never once did he pause, or even slow the pace.

Allegra struggled to clear her mind of fear, so that she could get her bearings. But all she could see in her mind's eye was the giant. Standing as tall as a tree. Hands big and rough and bruising as they bound her. And that one brief glimpse into his eyes. Eyes filled with utter darkness.

How had he bested the dragon? Could it be that this giant was even stronger than the mighty creature that stood guard over their kingdom? The thought terrified her.

The horse slowed to a walk and Allegra could hear the splash of water. Moments later she was shivering as the water soaked her bindings.

Her heart sank. This had to be the Enchanted Loch, the barrier that had always kept her and her family safe from the outside world. Once her abductor made it to the other side, he would be free to take her anywhere, and she would be unable to stop him.

She had to act now, or all would be lost.

Concentrating all her energy, she conjured an image of her mother, and as the image came into focus, called out to her in her mind.

Nola sat at her loom, pleased with the design she was weaving. At her feet sat Bessie. Despite the old woman's fearsome looks, she was a gentle soul who had long ago forgiven those who had mocked and reviled her. In gratitude for the haven she'd been given here in the Mystical Kingdom, she was devoted to Nola and her family.

The fabric on Nola's loom looked as though it

had been spun by angels. Soft as a spider's web it was, with fine, intricate spirals that looped one into the other like exotic jewels.

Old Bessie smiled. "This will make a lovely gown for one of your daughters."

"Aye. I so enjoy making them pretty things."

"And why not?" Bessie's smile deepened. "They're fairer than any flowers."

At a cry Nola's head came up sharply. "Allegra?"

She looked around for her daughter. Seeing no one, she glanced at the old woman. "Did you hear that?"

"Nay. But then I don't have your gifts, Nola."

At that Nola shoved away from the loom and walked to the door of the cottage.

Outside, Wilona was stirring her stew over an open fire.

"Allegra just called to me. Have you seen her?"

"Aye. Weeding her garden." Wilona's sharp eyes narrowed on her daughter's troubled face. "What's wrong?"

"Something, though I know not what." Already Nola was hurrying up the hill toward the meadow. "She needs me, for I heard her calling my name."

Wilona set aside her wooden spoon and hurried after her daughter, with the old woman trailing slowly behind.

When they came to the meadow, Nola knelt and retrieved the hoe from the dirt where Allegra had dropped it.

Her mother was already examining the print of a man's boot in the sand. Her tone was low with fear. "An intruder from beyond. He would have to slay the dragon." Wilona frowned in concentration. "I thought I heard a cry earlier, but because I was surrounded by bleating lambs, I couldn't be certain just what it was."

"Is he a barbarian?" Nola's tone was little more than a whisper.

"Nay." Wilona straightened, holding a torn piece of plaid that clung to a section of wattle fence. "A Highlander, from the look of this."

"No Highlander would dare to risk the Enchanted Loch."

"No ordinary Highlander, perhaps." Wilona caught her daughter's arm. "You must know that even hidden here, away from prying eyes, there are those who desire the power."

"But for what reason?"

The older woman shook her head. "I know not. But this I know. We must stop him before he crosses the loch, or all will be lost."

The two women lifted their fingers to their mouths and gave a series of shrill whistles. Within minutes Kylia stepped from the stream and hurried to the

meadow. From out of the forest came tiny Gwenellen, moving as swiftly as a shadow, followed more
slowly by Jeremy.

After a hasty explanation, the four women formed
a circle and joined hands, chanting in an ancient
tongue, while Jeremy and Bessie sat in the grass,
adding their voices to the chorus.

Merrick MacAndrew had never seen anything like
this. One minute the waters of the loch were so clear
and calm, he could see all the way to the bottom.
The next they were swirling and churning as though
they were a bubbling cauldron stirred by a witch's
spell.

Witch. His eyes narrowed on the bundle in his
arms. She may have looked like a goddess in her
garden, with that exquisite gown and hair neatly
plaited in one fat braid, but now he had no doubt
that this fiery female was the reason for the loch's
abrupt upheaval.

If he weren't so desperate, he'd have the sense to
be afraid. If his life meant anything at all to him, he
would surely turn back. But without his son, his life
was meaningless. And without the woman in his
arms, his son would surely die.

"Witch. You'll not deter me from my path," he
muttered.

Just then the angry waves swept him from the

saddle and he found himself floundering in the deep. For a moment his precious bundle was torn from his hands, but he managed to snag an end of the plaid and drag her close.

Coughing and choking, Allegra struggled against the cloth that bound her. "You must set me free at once."

"So you can flee? I'll see you dead before I consent to such foolishness."

"Then you'll have your wish soon enough." She coughed and came up sputtering as another wave washed over her. "At least give me an opportunity to stay afloat."

He was about to refuse when a thought came to him. "Aye. I'll do as you ask." Within seconds he'd unwrapped the length of plaid, freeing her hands and legs. Then, just as quickly, he wound it around his own waist and around hers, binding her firmly to him. "As long as you understand that in order to save your own life, you must save mine, as well." He shot her a look of triumph. "If one of us dies, the other dies, as well."

"You're mad."

"So I've been told."

A series of waves rolled over them, tumbling them about like leaves in a storm. But the cloth held, and when they came up, gasping for air, they were still bound together.

Seeing a flash of movement beside him, Merrick's arm shot out and he captured a handful of his horse's mane. His other arm wrapped around her as he shouted, ''Hold on, woman.''

They were dragged through the waves with such force they couldn't catch their breath. The water thrashed and pummeled and hurled them about until they were dazed and clinging. Each time they thought they'd survived the worst, the waves would increase in strength, battering them until they were struggling for breath.

Above the sound of the waves and water, Allegra heard the familiar words of the ancient chant and knew that her family had come together to try to save her. The thought of them forming a circle of protection gave her a sense of peace. As she was buffeted and tossed about, she closed her eyes, willing herself into the circle with them.

Suddenly a wall of water as high as the rock cliffs that surrounded the loch bore down on them, rolling them over and over until they were bruised and battered, their lungs screaming for air.

So this was how it felt to die, Allegra thought as she was dragged to the very bottom of the loch, still bound to the stranger. She absorbed a blow from the horse's flailing hooves as the terrified animal struggled to the surface.

For a moment she feared her head would explode

from the pain. Then she felt wave after wave of darkness rolling over her. Strong arms surrounded her, and she saw the face of her long-dead father, who had descended from the noblest of Scotland's families. Kenneth Drummond could trace his lineage all the way to the first king of the Scots.

She held on to him, thrilling to his strength as, with powerful strokes, he broke the surface. For several long moments they clung, filling their lungs with precious air. Then he untied the plaid and lifted her in his arms, carrying her to shore.

The water here was as calm as glass.

She lifted a hand to his cheek. "Am I dead then, Father?"

"You're neither dead, nor with your father."

At the sound of that stern voice, she opened her eyes and felt her heart plummet. Not her father. The giant.

He had somehow escaped the perils of the Forest of Darkness and the Enchanted Loch to storm the Mystical Kingdom itself.

Sweet heaven. Who was this man, that he could overcome such powerful magic?

In the meadow of the Mystical Kingdom a dark shadow passed overhead. A sudden wind came up, catching their hair and sending the hems of their gowns whipping about their ankles. The nearby trees were bent nearly double from the force of the wind.

Their chanting abruptly ceased as they looked around with a feeling of dread.

It was Wilona who finally spoke. "Allegra is lost to us. She is no longer safe within the confines of the Mystical Kingdom. Her captor's powers must be far more potent than ours. Or perhaps his need greater than ours."

"But how can that possibly be?" Gwenellen's eyes, as blue as sapphires, went wide with disbelief as she looked to her mother for the answer. "Why can't we cast a spell to stop him?"

"Come here, child." Nola drew her youngest daughter close, then caught her middle daughter's hand in hers. "There are two powers that are stronger than any other." Nola remembered the man who had claimed her heart, and had given her three precious daughters. "One is love." She thought of the myths and fears and gossip that had driven them from their home to seek refuge here in this place. "The other hate."

"How will we know which power drives Allegra's captor?" Kylia's dark eyes, usually flashing with humor, were now sparkling with tears.

Nola shook her head. "It is not for us to know."

"Then how can we help her?" Gwenellen's voice nearly caught in her throat.

Nola dropped an arm around each of her daughters' shoulders and drew them close to press kisses to their cheeks. "We can send Allegra calming thoughts and healing light to see her through whatever the fates have in store for her. Though your sister is unaccustomed to the ways of that other world beyond our shore, she is strong and brave. Best of all, there is a goodness in her heart that will see her through whatever trials may be in store for her."

But though Nola spoke with conviction, there was a heaviness around her own heart. She had brought her daughters here to protect them from a world of disbelievers. Now her beloved Allegra had been taken away from all that was safe and familiar, and thrust back into that very world.

A world that could use her innocence and tenderness against her.

A world that seemed always bent upon destroying that which it couldn't understand.

Chapter Two

Allegra lay on the banks of the Enchanted Loch, taking in deep gulps of air. As her breathing gradually slowed, she became aware of a dull ache at the side of her head. Touching a hand to the spot, she felt the swelling where the horse's hoof had grazed her. Any closer and she would have been knocked senseless.

Closing her eyes, she took deep, calming breaths while tracing her thumbs in gentle circles around and around her temple until the swelling disappeared, leaving only a small bruise. That effort cost her, and she was so exhausted she was forced to lie very still, until her strength gradually returned.

Feeling the warmth of sunlight on her closed lids, she opened her eyes. A short distance away the horse, drained from the exertion to stay afloat, had staggered about before stumbling to its knees. It struggled in the grass, eyes wide with fear, powerful chest heaving. The poor creature was confused, disoriented and absolutely terrified.

Overcome with tenderness, Allegra forced herself from her lethargy and crawled to the animal, laying her hands on its head. Almost at once the horse's breathing slowed, and its eyes seemed to focus on her with something akin to understanding.

Minutes later the horse scrambled to its feet and walked a short distance away, nibbling grass as though nothing had happened.

Merrick lay where he'd dropped on shore, watching all this through narrowed eyes. It was as he'd heard. This woman did indeed possess the power to heal. If he'd had any doubts before, they were now wiped away.

When she turned from the horse, Merrick was already on his feet facing her, pointing the tip of his sword at her heart. "Don't move, woman."

She looked up at him and saw again the darkness in his eyes. It was impossible to see into this man's soul. It was as though he'd closed a door, allowing no light in, allowing nothing of himself to escape.

Desperate, she turned her full gaze on the jewels winking in the sword's hilt. Within moments they glowed with a blinding fire that equaled the sun.

Merrick let out a hiss of pain as the fire burned into his palm, and he was forced to drop his weapon.

Allegra used that moment of distraction to turn and run. As she raced through the brush, her wet gown clung to her legs, slowing her progress. Tree branches snagged at her hair and arms, but she ignored the sting of pain and continued running until the breath burned her lungs.

From behind strong fingers clawed at her shoulders and she was yanked off her feet. She landed on the floor of the forest and looked up to find the giant standing over her, breathing heavily.

She struggled to keep the fear from her tone. "What is it you want of me? Why did you risk your life to come to the Mystical Kingdom?"

His fingers closed around her upper arms, dragging her to her feet. When she dug in her heels he simply tossed her over his shoulder and continued walking as though she weighed no more than a feather.

When they reached his waiting horse he pulled himself onto his steed's back and settled her in front of him. "You'll accompany me to my fortress."

"For what reason?"

With his arms firmly around her, he took the reins and nudged his horse into a gallop. As he ducked a low-hanging branch he brought his mouth close to her ear. "You will save my son, who is gravely ill."

She looked over her shoulder in alarm. "I can try. But many things are beyond my power."

He gave a quick shake of his head. "Hold your tongue, woman. I'll not listen to your feeble protestations of weakness, for I've had a taste of your strength. Know this. Whatever fate the lad suffers, so shall you. If he lives, I give you my word, I will return you to your people unharmed. If he dies, you will never see your home again, for you will join him in death. You'd be wise to heed this warning. My justice will be swift and sure."

Allegra shivered as the wind whipped her hair and stung her eyes. She could feel the darkness closing around her, chilling her blood. Could almost taste the bitterness that lay like a festering wound around this man's heart.

She was in the clutches of a madman. And she feared that regardless of the fate of this man's son, she was already doomed.

Merrick looked down at the woman in his arms. Now that sleep had finally claimed her, he was free to study her without her knowledge.

The bruise that had marred her temple was already fading, though just hours ago she'd had a lump the size of a hen's egg.

She didn't look like a witch. In fact, if he didn't know about her, he would think her a high-born woman. She was a rare beauty, with that unblemished skin lightly bronzed by sunlight, and hair the color of flame. When first he'd seen her working in her garden, her hair had been neatly plaited in a fat braid that fell below her waist. Now her encounter with the stormy loch had tossed her hair into wild disarray. It spilled around her like a veil, skimming the backs of his hands like wisps of finest silk.

Her gown was still damp, clinging to her body like a second skin. It was woven of exotic cloth that seemed more suitable for royalty. His gaze was drawn to the opening at her neckline, and the darkened cleft between high, firm breasts. The rush of heat to his loins caught him by surprise. Since Catherine, no woman had caused him even the slightest interest. But then, he told himself, this wasn't a woman. She was a witch. It was only natural that she would try to ensnare him in one of her spells.

His fingers tightened on the reins and he nudged his horse into a run. Let the witch sleep if she chose. As for him, he was driven by but one desire. To get her to his fortress as quickly as possible.

As the horse's hooves beat a steady tattoo along the rock-strewn forest trail, he whispered one thought like a litany.

Please. Let me be in time to save Hamish.

The loss of Catherine had been painful enough. Without his son, he would prefer death to the life of unending pain he knew would be his.

* * *

Allegra awoke to the sound of shouting. She glanced around in confusion, trying to make sense of the many strange sights. The Highland meadow looked much like the one in her Mystical Kingdom. Fields of heather waving in the breeze. To one side a waterfall spilling down hundreds of feet into a rushing stream. In the distance, tidy little cottages, and in the fields, flocks of sheep grazing on hillsides. But here were so many people. Men on horseback, others driving teams pulling wagons filled with hay and grain. Women staring down from upper windows, or glancing up from their chores as they wielded buckets and brooms, often with chubby infants at their hips. Children chasing each other around in fields, many of them pausing to stare at the man and woman as they passed.

"What is this place?"

"The village is called Berkshire. My home is Berkshire Castle." He pointed, and Allegra could see the turrets in the distance.

"A castle. Are you a lord?"

"I am." He spoke the words abruptly, as though they were distasteful to him. "Lord Merrick MacAndrew."

As they made their way through the village Allegra could see the people watching. But though they seemed respectful enough, they held their si-

lence. No one called or waved. There were no greet-
ings exchanged between the lord and his people.

Was their silence due to the fact that they shared
his fear for the life of his son? Or was there more
going on here?

She sensed one emotion stronger than the others
among these strangers. Fear. Of her? Or of their
lord?

Puzzled, Allegra sat up straighter as they approached the place Merrick MacAndrew called
home. Berkshire Castle was a natural fortification,
built high on a hilly piece of land, making a secret
approach impossible. With its back to the mountain,
there was but a single way to enter the portals.

As they drew closer, Allegra thought it an impos-
ing structure, with its high towers and guards posted
at the gates. Once they were inside the courtyard, a
pack of dogs set up a ferocious barking. As Merrick
stepped down from his steed they circled his feet,
tails wagging, tongues lolling. He reached up and
lifted Allegra from the back of the horse. Seeing the
way she shrank from them, he issued a sharp command and they fell silent.

Gingerly she reached down to touch the ruff of a
dog's neck, but quickly stepped back when it bared
its fangs and snarled.

Even the dogs, it seemed, were ill-tempered here
in this place.

"M'lord." The door opened and the housekeeper stepped out. "Praise heaven, you're alive. The rumors have been..." She stopped, then tried again. "I see you've brought..." She stared at Allegra as if seeing a ghost.

"I've brought the healer." To Allegra he said, "Mistress MacDonald is housekeeper here at Berkshire Castle."

Under other circumstances, the sight of the old woman would have brought a smile to Allegra's lips, for she was no bigger than a child. The hem of her dress brushed the ground. The apron encircled her tiny waist two or three times, and was held in place by an enormous sash.

Merrick's tone was abrupt. "Is there news of Hamish?"

The old woman shook her head sadly.

Merrick closed a hand around Allegra's wrist. "There's no need to prepare a chamber for this woman. Until my son recovers, she will not be allowed to leave his side." His tone fell, for Allegra's ears alone. "Don't bother with any of your tricks, woman, for you'll never be out of my sight."

The housekeeper paled and backed away as they started toward her. When Allegra walked past her the old woman crossed herself and grasped the door for support.

Once inside, Allegra had a quick impression of

soaring ceilings and great wooden stairs. Of tapestries lining the walls, and hundreds of candles blazing in chandeliers overhead. A dark space filled with gloom that no light seemed to penetrate. The oppression of this place weighed heavily on her.

There was no time to look around or sort through the source of the darkness, as Merrick kept a tight hold on her wrist, hauling her quickly up the stairs and along a hallway until he opened a door to a chamber.

Once they were inside a servant looked startled before making a quick bow and slipping away, leaving Merrick and his captive staring at the pale figure in the bed.

"This is my son, Hamish. He took a fall and later became feverish. Since then, he hasn't left his bed. Heal him."

Instead of obeying, she merely looked down at the lad. So pale. So still. "How long ago did this happen?"

Merrick shrugged. "A week. Perhaps two."

Allegra arched a brow. "So long. And where were you, my lord?"

His scowl deepened. "On the field of battle. Dispatching invaders. When I returned home and learned of this, I vowed to find someone who could save him. Now do it."

They both looked up at the sound of hurried footsteps. A tall, sandy-haired man paused on the threshold. His eyes widened in surprise. "Merrick? Cousin, the servants told me you were back." His eyes narrowed suspiciously. "Don't tell me you actually reached the Mystical Kingdom and lived to tell about it?"

"I'll tell you everything later, Mordred. Right now I must see to the healer."

Another man lumbered through the doorway and stood gaping at Allegra. Taller even than Merrick, his shoulders wider than a broadsword, he appeared to have hastily thrown on his tunic, which was unfastened, and his boots, which hadn't been laced. To Allegra he was truly frightening to behold. His eyes seemed vacant. His speech, when he finally found his voice, was that of a child. "You're back, cousin?"

"Aye, Desmond. With the healer."

Allegra shivered as the three men studied her. There was darkness here. Evil. It seemed to be all around her. It was new to her. And frightening. She'd heard about the darkness that could poison a man's heart and soul. But until now it had been something she'd heard about only from her mother and grandmother.

Merrick's tone deepened. "You heard me, woman. See to my son."

Struggling to ignore the men, Allegra turned her

back on them and sat on the edge of the lad's pallet, placing her hands on either side of his head. At once she felt the heat of his fever rush through her, almost searing her flesh.

She closed her eyes, trying to sort through the jumble of images that flitted through his mind and into hers. So many people and events moving through his young mind. It left her weak, and more than a little dazed.

"Who is the beautiful golden-haired lady who hovers nearby?"

Desmond gasped and turned to his brother, who cautioned him to be silent.

Merrick's face twisted into a ravaged mask. "You see Hamish's mother?"

"If she has eyes the color of the sky, and a half-moon scar above one brow, then I saw his mother for a moment before she disappeared." Allegra fell silent, attempting to concentrate, despite the distractions. There was such heat here. It was much more than mere fever. But what stoked this fire? Fear? Dread? An evil potion?

"I'll need willow bark. Essence of balm. Wood anemone, and cool water from a Highland stream."

Merrick struggled to rein in his impatience. "I saw you heal yourself, as well as my steed, with nothing more than a touch. What need have you of these things?"

"There is more here than a fever. More than a mere tumble from a tree. Your son lies gravely ill, my lord. Do you wish him cured, or merely brought back from the edge of death?"

Without warning his hands closed around her upper arms, dragging her to her feet. His face, inches from hers, was tight with fury, his breath hot against her cheek.

"I didn't risk life and limb to spar with your tart tongue, woman. You'll get everything you need. But never forget, if I find you playing me for a fool, I'll see that you pay dearly."

He released her and turned on his heel, shouting for the housekeeper, who came running.

"Our healer desires willow bark, essence of balm, wood anemone and cool water. See that they are brought to her at once."

"Aye, my lord."

He turned to Allegra, who hadn't moved. "Will you require anything else?"

"That's enough. For now." Trembling from his touch, she turned her back on him and settled herself once more beside the boy. She knew if she were to check, she would find bruises on her upper arms. The lord's hands were strong enough that he could easily snap her bones with but a single touch.

There was such violence in him. Though he kept it in check, it was there, bubbling just beneath the surface, threatening at any moment to boil over, scalding anyone who got too close.

Was his anger the cause of so much darkness in this place? Or had the darkness caused his anger?

She needed to put aside her fear of the lord if she were to open herself to the needs of his son. Still, it was disconcerting to have the man here, hovering about, weighing her every move. He was a distraction. One she could ill afford, especially since she was having such trouble concentrating.

The lad's mother was no longer in the land of the living, but was now on the other side. Of that Allegra was certain. But from the troubled look in her eyes, it had not been a peaceful passing. Perhaps, Allegra thought suddenly, the lord had had a hand in her death. That would explain why she hovered so near, wishing to protect her son from the same cruel fate.

Allegra laid her hands on the lad's head and closed her eyes, struggling to shut out the man and his problems while absorbing the boy's pain. At once she was thrust back into a Highland meadow. She had a sense of the boy's voice, high-pitched with excitement. Hamish climbing. Laughing as, surefooted as a mountain cat, he moved from branch to branch. Allegra felt the momentary distraction. Was it a flash of memory? Something or someone just above him, hidden in the branches? Whether it was man or beast, it seemed dark and frightening. Had he been startled? Pushed?

She probed deeper. The glint of murky liquid in a silver goblet. A muffled gasp. Then the image was gone and there was a quick little skitter of fear as the lad's foot slipped, and he realized he'd lost his grip. Then he was tumbling, head over heels, toward the ground.

She absorbed the jolt as he landed in the grass and lay watching the sky above him spinning in dizzying circles. Allegra felt the room spin and wanted desperately to press a hand to her stomach. But she dared not let go of the lad now, when they were so closely connected.

Again something. A flash of memory. A face peering down at him. A whispered voice that sent icy chills along the lad's spine. Then, before he could hold on to it, the memory was gone.

Ever so slowly the clouds came into focus, and then he was struggling to sit up.

Allegra's own mind settled.

"Hamish?" It was a feminine voice. "Are you hurt?"

"Nay." He got to his feet.

"Want to climb again?"

He shook his head. "I must go home."

"Not yet. Come. We'll climb higher."

"Nay." He refused, though he knew not why. He

knew only that he had to go home. Now. This instant, while the fear had him by the throat. He struggled for a reason. "Mistress MacDonald said Cook was making biscuits the way I like them. Drizzled with honey. I mustn't be late."

Hamish started toward his father's fortress in the distance.

Allegra wondered at the sudden flare of heat as the boy had another flash of memory. Just a flash, but it was enough to cause a spark of absolute terror. The spark flared into flame, burning so brightly it obscured all thought but one.

Danger. Danger. He had to get home at once.

Then he was running. Running so hard, so fast, his heart was thundering, and the breath burning his throat. There was but one thought Allegra could discern. He had to get to his father's home. There was something important he had to tell him as soon as he returned from the battle. His very life, and that of everyone here in the castle, depended on it.

Allegra looked up at a commotion in the doorway as the housekeeper directed servants to set up a table beside the boy's pallet. At once the connection was broken, and the boy's thoughts scattered and fled and were lost to her. She took in several deep breaths to calm her racing heart.

"We fetched what you've asked for." The tiny woman was out of breath from her hasty climb.

"Thank you." Allegra sighed. Now she would have to begin again.

As she let go of the boy's hands and sat back, she glanced at the housekeeper and had to turn away to hide the sudden smile that threatened.

The poor woman was too terrified to enter the room. Instead she'd remained in the doorway, calling out her directions while holding on to the door. Perhaps, Allegra thought, she meant to slam it in her face if threatened with harm.

The servants looked equally afraid, working so quickly they nearly knocked each other over in their desire to escape.

At least, she thought, there would be few interruptions. Except, of course, for Lord Merrick MacAndrew. He was now pacing back and forth in front of the fire, a goblet of ale in his hands.

He paused to stare at her, and she felt as though she were staring down the devil himself. Such anger there. Such darkness.

He drained his goblet, then resumed his pacing.

It was then she noticed that his cousins, Mordred and Desmond, had also remained. Both men were seated in the shadows, their gazes narrowed on her with fierce concentration. Perhaps they thought to protect the lord from the wicked witch.

This was, she feared, going to prove to be a very long night. And with each passing minute, she could feel her strength ebbing.

Chapter Three

Allegra was grateful that the others had finally vacated the lad's chambers. Now her only distraction was Merrick MacAndrew, who hovered over her like an avenging angel.

She ground the willow bark into a fine powder, then sprinkled it into a goblet of water before holding it to the lad's lips.

At once Merrick was beside her, clamping a hand on her wrist. "Hold, woman. What is this thing you give my son?"

"A potion for the fever."

"Before it passes his lips, you will taste it."

She was already shaking her head. "I have no need…"

His fingers tightened on her flesh. "I said, you're to drink first."

"Very well." She took a taste. "And now will

you waste precious hours waiting to see if I die, before allowing me to minister to the lad?''

Merrick's frustration came out in a hiss of breath. ''Enough of your insolence, woman. See to him.''

Very gently she held the goblet to the boy's lips and watched with satisfaction until it was empty. Then she turned her attention to the balm and wood anemone, grinding each into powder.

With each twist of her hand, as she worked mortar and pestle, she could feel her strength being drained.

Merrick studied the concoctions with a wary look. ''What do you hope to do with these weeds?''

''They are herbs. Wood anemone alleviates swelling. As for the sweet balm, I'll use it to help the lad sort through his thoughts. He seems confused.''

Merrick's eyes narrowed. ''You've read his thoughts?''

''That is not my gift. But there are a few thoughts mingled with the pain, which I can discern. Perhaps it is the blow to the head, or perhaps there is something that is still causing him such fear, it blocks all else, even the healing.''

Merrick's voice lowered with feeling. ''Can he hear my voice?''

For the first time since encountering this angry man, Allegra saw a glimmer of the depth of his pain, something he'd managed to keep from her until now. "I know not. Who can say what those on the other side can hear?"

"The other side?" He blanched. "Is he dead, then?"

"Nay, my lord." Seeing his pallor, Allegra was quick to explain. "He is not dead, but he has slipped far away from this life."

"Why?" The word came out in a croak of misery.

"Some go there because it is a place of healing. Others go to prepare themselves for a life far different from the one they know here."

"You'll not let him go, do you understand?" Again his fingers tightened on her wrist, and she felt the mixture of anger and frustration pulsing through him. "Cast a spell, or do whatever it takes to keep him with me. If you fail, woman, you know what will happen."

"Aye." She snatched her hand away. "You've made that perfectly clear, my lord. Now I suggest you tend to your son."

"Tend him? How?"

"Speak to him, as a father speaks to his son. Call to him. Let him know you are here, waiting to welcome him back from his sojourn to that other place. Urge him to come back to you."

For a moment Merrick merely glowered at her. Then, putting aside his anger at the woman, he knelt beside the bed and touched a hand to the lad's forehead.

His voice, when he finally spoke, vibrated with feeling. "Hamish, lad. I'm here now. Nothing can harm you, son. Nothing. Let go of your fears and come back to me. Please, Hamish. I need you here with me. You're all I have in this world now."

Allegra stood to one side, watching and listening in amazement. When Merrick MacAndrew spoke to his son, he became a different man. The brute who would force his will on others disappeared beneath the guise of a loving father. But she sensed that this was no mere playacting. The love this man felt for his son was a living, palpable thing.

Still, she would do well to remember that this was no gentle lord, but a coarse brute. And she had the bruises to prove it.

Shivering, she walked to the fire and stood with hands outstretched. But even this close, the warmth eluded her. The dizzy feeling that had come over her when she'd touched the lad was with her still. She felt light as air. As though, unless she anchored herself, she would float clear up to the rough wooden beams of the ceiling.

She took hold of the back of a chair and went very still, struggling to keep her wits about her. But now there was a strange buzzing in her head, and little stars began floating in front of her eyes. Bright they were, and giving off sparks that blinded her. It was unlike anything she'd ever experienced before.

As if from a great distance she heard the lord's voice calling to her. "What are you about now, woman? I'll have none of your tricks. Come here and see to my son."

She wanted to answer him. But though she opened her mouth, no words came out. Instead, the room went suddenly dark. She felt herself tumbling down into a deep, black abyss.

Strong arms caught and held her before she could fall to the floor. She felt herself being lifted and cradled against a solid wall of chest. She had not the strength to lift so much as a hand in her defense as she was lowered to a pallet.

There were voices. So many voices around her, and all of them babbling.

The high-pitched voice of the housekeeper. "Well, m'lord, no wonder the poor lass fainted. How long has it been since you fed her?"

The impatient tone of her captor cut through. "There was no time for food, Mistress MacDonald."

"No time for food? And what about dry clothes?" Something tugged on Allegra's boots, and she felt warm fingers rolling away her cold, wet stockings. "Look at her. Soaked to the skin. Ye must leave now, m'lord. 'Twouldn't be proper for ye to stay here while I strip away her clothes and wrap her in dry linen.''

"I have no intention of letting this woman out of my sight until Hamish is healed.''

A long, deep sigh, and then the resigned notes of the housekeeper. "Very well, m'lord. But to preserve her modesty, ye will walk to the balcony until I've dressed her in a dry night shift.''

Allegra heard the sounds of booted feet storming across the room, and then the soft rustling as the housekeeper began removing her wet gown and undergarments.

When Allegra's eyes opened the old woman took a step back, her face registering shock, then fear, then resignation. Pressing her lips together, she returned to the bedside, determined to complete her task.

Allegra touched a hand to her head. "I've never…fainted before.''

"Ye've no doubt never gone this long without eating before, I'll wager. I've sent a serving wench to fetch some broth and biscuits.''

"Thank you, Mistress MacDonald.''

The housekeeper's lips curved into a lopsided smile. "Up close ye don't look like a witch. Why, ye're hardly more than a lass.''

"I'm ten and nine. By the time my mother was my age, she had three babes."

"As did I. I was wed when I was but ten and three." The old woman helped her into a soft, warm night shift, before draping her in a shawl for modesty. "This'll warm ye."

"Thank you." Allegra looked around. "Where am I?"

"Ye're still in the lad's chamber. I've made up a pallet for ye near his." She lowered her voice. "The lord wouldn't hear of ye leaving the lad's bedside."

"You're very kind, Mistress MacDonald."

The old woman shook her head. "Ye're here to heal our dear Hamish. For that, I'll do whatever I can to see to ye'r comfort, lass."

"Even though you're afraid of me?"

The housekeeper gave her a sideways glance. "Are ye reading my mind?"

Allegra laughed, a clear lilting sound. "There's no need to do that, Mistress MacDonald. You're not very good at hiding your feelings."

"Are ye a witch, lass?"

Allegra's smile faded. "Perhaps. I don't know."

"Isn't that why ye live in the Mystical Kingdom? To keep ye'r secrets from the rest of us mortals?"

Allegra shook her head. "The Mystical Kingdom has been home to our clan for hundreds of years. I've been there since I was very young. My mum and gram say we took refuge there because the outside world fears and reviles what it cannot understand. There are many who would punish us for being different.''

''What is ye'r name, lass?''

''Allegra. Allegra of the clan Drummond.''

''Ah. 'Tis an ancient and honorable clan, Allegra Drummond.''

When a shadow fell over the bed both women looked up. From the scowl on Merrick MacAndrew's face, Allegra had no doubt that he'd overheard everything.

''I see you're well enough to gossip with my housekeeper. Does this mean you're well enough now to see to the lad?''

Mistress MacDonald crossed her arms over her chest. ''I've ordered broth and biscuits for the lass. And Cook has prepared a meal for ye in the great hall, m'lord, where Mordred and Desmond await ye.''

''Tell Cook I'll take my meal here, Mistress MacDonald.''

''Here?'' She glanced around. ''But the lass...''

''Is here at my pleasure. She will sup with me. And then, when her strength is restored, she will do what she was brought here to do.''

''Aye, m'lord.'' The old woman gave a worried

glance at Allegra before hurrying off to see that the lord's orders were carried out.

When the housekeeper returned, she was trailed by half a dozen servants. While two of them set a table in front of the fireplace, laying it with fine linen, crystal and silver, the others were busy setting an array of food on a sideboard.

When all was in readiness the old woman sent the servants scurrying before announcing, "Ye'r dinner is served, m'lord. Will ye have ale?"

"I will. And so will the woman. It will help warm her."

"Aye, m'lord." After filling two goblets, she stood beside the table. "I'll just wait and serve ye'r food."

"There's no need, Mistress MacDonald. You're needed in the great hall. Fill our plates with a variety of Cook's fine food. If we want more, we can serve ourselves."

"Aye, m'lord." After doing as he asked, the old woman gave a last worried glance at Allegra before bustling from the room.

When she was gone, Merrick startled Allegra by lifting her from her pallet.

She shrank back. "What are you doing?"

"I don't want you fainting on me again." His warm breath feathered the hair at her temple, sending the most amazing curls of pleasure along her spine. For the first time in hours she felt warm, all the way to her toes.

She didn't know what to do with her arms. To keep them from encircling his neck, she clasped her hands together tightly. Because he was holding her so close, her face rested naturally against the warm hollow of his throat. She breathed in the unfamiliar scent of him, and found it so potent it went straight to her head.

This was a different kind of dizziness. Though her mind seemed to spin in lazy circles, she felt strangely focused. And though one part of her wanted to move away, another, stronger part of her wanted to remain just this way.

She'd never been held by a man before, except for her father. But he hadn't lived long enough for her to remember much about him, except in dreams. Before, when Merrick had held her astride his horse, she'd been too afraid to allow the sensations to sink in. Now it wasn't fear she was experiencing, but something far different. Something so alien, she would need time and distance to sort it out.

"You'll sit here." He lowered her onto a fur-draped chaise set before the fire.

Once he released her, he reached for a goblet of ale and handed it to her. "This, and the fire, will have you warm in no time."

He circled the table and took the seat across from

her before picking up his own goblet and drinking. Allegra did the same, feeling the warmth of the ale seep into her veins.

Though her shift of white lawn was modest enough, with a high rounded neckline and long, tapered sleeves, it couldn't hide the lithe young body beneath. Even the shawl draped about her shoulders couldn't hide the swell of breasts. The bare feet peeking out from beneath her long skirts made Merrick aware that, except for the shift, she wore nothing.

It wasn't an image he'd invited, but now that it was here in his mind, he couldn't seem to get past it.

He set down his goblet and stared at her in a way that had her heart thundering. Then he blinked and the look was gone. Or had she only imagined it?

She bent to her food. After several bites of mutton she looked up and smiled. "This is grand. I think it may be as good as my gram's."

"I take it that's meant as a compliment?"

"Aye. My gram can make biscuits that melt in the mouth, and cook fish from the loch that would make you weep."

"Has she taught you her secrets?"

Allegra shook her head. "She tries. But she often complains that, though my sisters and I have many gifts, cooking isn't one of them. Then there is Jeremy. He's a little troll who lives with us, because he had no other home.''

"I've heard trolls are nasty creatures.''

She shook her head. "Jeremy isn't like that, though he may have been at one time. Now he simply enjoys the beauty of the Mystical Kingdom.''

"What of your sisters? Are they healers, too?''

Allegra looked down. "We are all gifted, though in different ways. I'm the best healer, though the others can manage simple wounds. Kylia can also see the past, and on occasion, look into the future. What's even more impressive, she can look into a man's heart and see good or evil. Then there's Gwenellen…'' Just the thought of her youngest sister had Allegra smiling. "She has not yet discovered her gifts, though I'm certain she will in time.''

Merrick seemed most interested in Kylia's gift. "You say your sister can look in a man's heart. What if she sees both good and evil?''

"She would see both, but would not judge him. Kylia is far too sweet to ever judge another.''

"And what of you, Allegra?'' The name rolled off his tongue like honey and startled him for a moment, for it was the first time he'd said it aloud. His tone softened. "Are you sweet like your sister, or are you a witch to be feared?''

She looked up, and he felt the smoldering heat of her anger. "Are you like all the others, my lord?

Eager to use my gift when it suits your purpose, then resorting to cruel names to brand me different?''

He reached for his goblet, avoiding her eyes. Her words were too close to the mark, and shamed him. But he'd be damned if he'd ask forgiveness of this…this tart-tongued female. ''We waste time talking, woman. We'll eat, and then you can return your attention to my son.''

Allegra shivered as the cold settled into her bones once more. Whatever tenuous truce they'd attempted, it had dissolved like the wisps of fog that often drifted over the Enchanted Loch until banished by the sun.

The man across the table was once more the demanding lord. And she, like it or not, his unwilling captive.

Chapter Four

Merrick sat brooding while Allegra finished her meal in stony silence. Why should he feel guilty for calling her a witch? Isn't that what she was? Still, she'd looked so hurt. A hurt that had now turned to stony anger. He couldn't help comparing that with the way she'd looked when she'd been speaking of her family. There had been such sweetness about her. A light had come into her eyes that made them glow as green as a Highland loch. And for a moment high color had bloomed on her cheeks, making her as fresh and colorful as the flowers in her garden.

It was natural that she missed her family. Didn't he miss his home whenever he was off fighting a battle? Of course, the choice to stay or leave was his alone to make, and she'd been given no such choice. But this was different. Fate had backed him to the wall and he'd had to fight his way out. If he felt a twinge of guilt about taking her far from her home, he quickly brushed it aside. He couldn't afford to care about anyone but Hamish. If the witch healed the lad, she would soon enough be back with her sisters in the Mystical Kingdom.

What a strange place it had been. Lush and green, with brilliant flowers that grew taller than a man and the air perfumed like a lover's chamber. It wasn't only the air that was sweeter. The light there had been touched with such amazing color, gilding everything with gold and precious jewels. Even the drops of water in the Enchanted Loch had glowed like pearls.

He'd caught glimpses of creatures there that he'd never seen anywhere else in the Highlands. Winged horses, small and delicate, yet big enough to carry a woman or child. At least, he'd thought they were horses. One minute he saw them, the next they vanished from his line of vision. He'd also spotted tiny fairies flitting through the tallest branches of the trees. He'd seen a halo of light around them, and had heard their voices, whispering and giggling. But like the horses, one minute they were there, the next they were gone, and he'd wondered if he'd actually seen and heard them, or if he'd only imagined it.

Then he'd caught sight of Allegra tending her garden, and he'd been oblivious to all else around him. At first he'd refused to believe what he saw. Why would a witch tend a garden in an enchanted land? Couldn't she simply command that the crops grow, and her wish would be granted? But there she was, lost in her work, giving him time to bask in her rare beauty.

Her gown of rich green, shot with gold threads, appeared to have been spun by angels. It had draped the most perfect body, all willow slender and softly rounded curves. Fiery hair hung down her back in one long fat braid, twined with green ribbons. On her feet had been dainty kid slippers. But the hoe in her hand had been plain and serviceable. And she'd worked it with all the fervor of a peasant. That only added to his fascination.

It seemed incongruous that one so lovely could work until her hands were calloused and blistered.

For a moment he'd been so taken by her beauty, he'd nearly fallen under her spell. But the thought of Hamish, and what he must do to save his son, had hardened his heart.

It had almost happened again just now when he'd carried her to the table. The press of that body to his had him thinking things that were better left alone. Thoughts of lying with her, of pleasuring himself with her, had been nearly overpowering. And when her mouth had barely skimmed his throat, he'd found himself drowning in sensations.

Even now she seemed a contradiction. All buttoned up in that prim night shift, while her hair flowed about her face and shoulders and spilled down her back like a veil of fire.

He would have to remember to protect his heart from this woman. After all, despite her pretense at innocence, this was no ordinary maiden. She would know every trick to steal a man's mind, his heart and finally his soul. For the sake of Hamish, Merrick knew he had to be strong.

He had no fear of her. After all, he was a seasoned warrior. He knew how to do battle against his enemy.

He looked up with a start when he realized that she'd spoken. "Forgive me. I was deep in thought."

She inclined her head. "I said now that Cook's fine meal has restored my strength, I'll do what you brought me here to do. It's time I saw to your son."

He pushed away from the table and snagged his ale before following her across the room. There he slouched in a chaise, his long legs crossed at the ankles, watching with keen interest as she perched on the edge of the boy's pallet.

She smoothed the balm over the lad's forehead, then gently lifted his head and spread more at the base of his skull.

Merrick felt his skin prickling, and found himself wondering what it would be like to have her touch him like that. He could almost feel those long, delicate fingers moving over him, caressing, arousing.

Annoyed, he put aside such thoughts to watch and learn the ways of this witch.

She touched her fingertips to Hamish's temples and closed her eyes. She remained that way for so long, Merrick began to wonder what it was she was feeling. Her expressive face showed such a range of emotions. One minute she was smiling, the next her brow furrowed into a frown of deep concentration. She was relaxed for the space of a heartbeat, and then her face was twisted in pain. So much pain.

Merrick felt a jolt of understanding. Could it be that she was experiencing everything the lad was experiencing?

Suddenly she opened her eyes, staring down at Hamish as she began to chant in an ancient tongue.

The words were meaningless to Merrick, but he found them oddly soothing. Her voice, naturally low in pitch, was mesmerizing. He had to fight the urge to close his eyes and let that rich voice wash over him. Instead he forced himself to study her every move with great care. If she appeared to threaten the lad in any way, he would be on her like an avenging angel.

Her eyes were fixed on Hamish's face with such unblinking intensity, they seemed to burn like points of flame. The ancient words poured out of her, as from one in a trance.

Abruptly she began speaking to the lad in his own tongue.

"I know you're torn, Hamish, between your desire to remain where you are, in the company of those who offer you comfort, and to return to the life you once enjoyed. You need have no fear. Whatever harm threatened you has been banished. Here in this place you're surrounded by people who love you and will look out for your comfort and your security. Your father is right here, eager to speak with you."

At that Merrick got to his feet and walked to the other side of the pallet, peering down at his son. Behind the closed lids he saw a wild fluttering, as though the lad were struggling against a bright light.

Allegra's voice remained low and soothing. "It's all right, Hamish. You can come back now. Come. See your father, who has been waiting such a long time to speak with you. Put his mind at rest now, Hamish. Come home to him."

Suddenly the lids rose, and the boy's eyes were open.

The goblet fell from Merrick's nerveless fingers, splashing ale across the floor as he dropped to his knees with a cry. "Oh, Hamish lad. You've come back to me."

With tears spilling down his cheeks he gathered the boy into his arms and pressed his face into his hair.

Allegra stepped away from the bedside, not only to give father and son the privacy they deserved, but also because the weakness was upon her again. And this time it wasn't because of a lack of food, or the difficult journey. She recognized this feeling from past experiences. It was simply the price she had to pay for having used her gift. Crossing over into that other side exacted a heavy toll upon the one who was the bridge.

At the dining table she sank onto a chair. Folding her arms on the tabletop, she rested her chin there, taking comfort in the sound of the lad's first halting words.

"You're...home...Father."

"Aye, Hamish."

"For how long? Just until the next battle?"

"I can't say, lad. We'll not speak of such things. For now, I'm home with you. And you're back with me." Merrick framed the boy's face and stared at him with naked hunger. "I feared I'd lost you, lad. Mistress MacDonald told me you fell from a tree."

"Did I?" The boy thought about it a moment before shaking his head. "I don't recall."

"It doesn't matter." His father wrapped him in

his arms and let out a long, deep sigh. "Nothing matters now that you're back with me, Hamish."

The two remained that way for the longest time, with Merrick rocking his son and crooning to him, and the boy holding on to him, taking comfort in his father's strength.

They looked up as the housekeeper came bustling into the room, followed by several servants. When she caught sight of father and son embracing, she let out a shout of joy.

"Praise heaven, m'lord. Is it truly our young Hamish, awake and smiling?"

"It is indeed, Mistress MacDonald."

Merrick beamed as the old woman touched the lad's face, as if to assure herself. Then she promptly burst into tears and had to lift her apron to dab at her eyes.

The servants gathered around, laughing and clapping the lad on the back. Soon, as the word spread, the entire household began spilling into the boy's chambers, eager to share in the good news.

Mordred and Desmond paused in the doorway.

"It's true, then." Mordred's booming voice had everyone glancing up as he strode forward to lean over the bed and clasp his cousin's hand. "The lad is back in the land of the living. Isn't he a welcome sight, Desmond?"

"Aye." Desmond squeezed the lad's shoulder.

Hamish pulled away and looked questioningly at his father, who merely gathered him close and rocked him in his big arms.

As more of the household gathered around, Merrick became puzzled by his son's reaction. Hamish had always been too bold for his own good, climbing without fear, leaping as though he could fly, without regard to the peril. He'd always refused to heed his parents' cautions, choosing instead to rush headlong through life.

Now he seemed overly shy. As timid as a cornered mouse.

Though the lad seemed pleased to see everyone, he also seemed wary, grasping his father's hand often. At times, when too many loomed over his pallet at once, he shrank back in fear.

It was, Merrick decided, merely the result of the injury. Soon enough it would pass and the lad would be as before.

He could see the excitement beginning to take its toll. When Hamish stifled a yawn and his lids began to droop, Merrick gave the word to his housekeeper to order the others to leave. At once the old woman shooed them away, though she couldn't bring herself to do the same. She lingered, brushing back the lad's hair from his forehead, patting his hand, repeating all the things she'd whispered to him during his long sleep.

"Ye're back with us now, lad. Truly back with those of us who love ye." More tears fell from her eyes. But these were happy tears, and her joy was so great she no longer bothered to wipe them away.

Merrick sat beside his son, basking in the glow of sheer relief. He turned to Mordred and Desmond, who had remained. "It's as if the weight of the world has been lifted from my shoulders."

"Aye." Mordred nodded. "You risked everything, and won the grandest prize of all. Neither the threat of monsters nor the fear of the unknown could keep you from finding the witch and bringing her here to weave her magic."

The witch.

Merrick looked around and saw that she was seated at the table, her face in her hands. Was she weeping?

He crossed to her and was startled to find her fast asleep. When he touched a hand to her shoulder, she didn't move.

Puzzled, he laid a hand over hers and drew back in surprise. She was so cold, so still, she could have been carved from stone.

Alarmed, he bent and lifted her into his arms. At once he could feel the cold seeping into him.

"Mistress MacDonald."

At his shout the old woman looked over, then

seeing the lord holding the lass in his arms, hurried to his side.

By this time he was trembling with cold. It was unlike anything he'd ever felt. It seemed to pass in waves through his body from the woman in his arms, leaving him chilled to the marrow of his bones. How was it possible for anyone to be this cold and still be alive?

Was she dying, then?

The thought left him suddenly terrified. What price had he exacted for the life of his son?

His voice was rough with impatience. "Have one of the servants stoke this fire, Mistress MacDonald. Then fetch me the strongest ale we have."

"What's wrong with the lass, m'lord?"

"I know not." He knelt and settled her on her pallet, carefully wrapping her in layers of fur. "She's so pale, so still. But see? When I touch a finger to her throat, I can feel the pulse there. Though it's little more than a feeble whisper, it gives me hope that she can be saved."

Mordred's tone was incredulous. "You can't mean it, Merrick. She isn't like the rest of us. You'd be wise to keep your distance, else you might find yourself bewitched by this creature. Is that what you want?"

"You know it isn't. But this I know. Because of this woman, I have my son back. Now I must do whatever I can to return the favor. If necessary, I'll move heaven and earth to see her safe.''

''This is madness.'' As Mordred and his brother followed the housekeeper from the chambers, he could be heard muttering under his breath about the fact that his cousin might have already been bewitched.

That had the old woman glancing over her shoulder at the lord, and had the servants murmuring among themselves over the dangerous creature that had been set loose among them.

Merrick seemed oblivious to their comments as he rubbed Allegra's hands between his while he whispered, ''If only I knew the magic that would restore you, lass, as you restored my Hamish.''

All through the night, while young Hamish slept peacefully, Merrick sat beside Allegra's pallet. Each time a servant entered the chambers to stoke the fire, Merrick would rouse himself to force several drops of ale between her lips.

Was it helping to ease the cold? He thought so. He closed a big hand around hers and wondered whether he actually detected some small change in her, or if he merely thought so because he wanted it to be so.

This woman was his responsibility. Except for him, she would still be living peacefully in her hidden kingdom. He would not, by heaven, desert her in her time of need.

And yet there seemed so little he could do. The fire, the ale, the nest of furs seemed useless against the icy fingers of death that held her in their grip.

At last, desperate to pull her back from this cold abyss, he did the only thing he could think of. He slipped beneath the furs and stretched out beside her, wrapping his arms around her, willing her the warmth of his own body.

Chapter Five

Allegra was lost in the Valley of Mist, shivering in the darkness. Wisps of fog danced across the loch and wrapped themselves around her like shrouds. She tried to see the sun, but her vision was clouded. She wanted to call for her winged horse to carry her home, but her voice was strangely silent.

Her power was depleted, leaving her weak and vulnerable. She was cold. So cold. Without her understanding family to minister to her, she was doomed. Soon the cold would penetrate her bones, snapping them like twigs. Her blood, too, would thicken and slow and then her heart, denied its precious fuel, would simply stop.

And yet, even knowing the price she would be forced to pay, how could she have denied the warrior his only child? She had seen the depth of his pain. Her heart had been touched by a father's desperate plea. Hadn't he risked his own life for that of the lad, defying the Enchanted Loch and the Mystical Kingdom to fetch her? She could do no less than that brave warrior. She had decided to defy the fates and give him his heart's desire.

And now she must pay the price. She remained paralyzed by the cold and, in her weakened condition, unable to stop its insidious destruction. She lifted her head to the sky and struggled to see the faces of her family, so far away.

At that moment something burned a path of fire down her throat. Her grandmother had once told her the kindness of a stranger was powerful magic. Allegra swallowed the heat gratefully and felt the first tiny flicker of hope.

As the hours passed and the cold closed around her once more, she was forced to swallow more fire. Then, just when the ice was threatening to take her down, the clouds parted and she saw a glimpse of the sun.

Warmth trickled through her. It was little more than a pinprick of light at first, but it was enough to lift her spirits. Perhaps, if she could hold onto the warmth, she could escape the Valley of Mist.

Something warm and strong wrapped itself around her, giving her the strength to go deep inside herself, searching for the light. And though it was faint and flickering, it was enough to sustain her. She held on to it with all her strength.

And slept.

Allegra awoke and lay very still, enjoying the precious warmth that enveloped her like a cocoon. Somehow, even without her family to minister to her, she had escaped the Valley of Mist. Because of someone's kindness, she had survived.

She listened to the steady beat of her heart and rejoiced at the sound. She was alive. Truly alive. Suddenly she became aware of a second heartbeat, keeping time with hers.

Her eyes snapped open. As she adjusted to the predawn gloom brightened only by the glowing embers on the hearth, she realized that she wasn't alone in her pallet. Strong arms enfolded her. Warm breath feathered the hair at her temple, sending heat curling along her spine.

"So." Merrick's voice was little more than a deep whisper that sent shivers along her spine. "You're awake at last."

It gave her an odd little jolt to know that he'd been watching her while she slept. "Why are you...?" She tried to pull away, but he held her firmly against the length of him. "Why are you here in my bed?"

"I knew of no other way to warm you."

"It was you?" Again the curl of heat along her spine at the knowledge that this man, whom she considered her enemy, had been the one to save her.

"You'd grown so cold I feared you were dead." He peered at her through narrowed eyes. "Were you?"

She shook her head. "Nay. I was...in another place."

"Not a warm and friendly place, from the looks of you. But no matter. Now you're back." Instead of moving away, he merely shifted, so that she had to put a hand to his chest to keep from being crushed against him.

He lifted a hand to brush a curtain of hair from her face. "Does this happen often, this going away to another place?"

At his touch she shivered, though this time it wasn't from the cold. In fact, with the mere brush of his hand, the heat increased.

She wondered how much she should tell him. After a moment's hesitation she said, "It happens only when I'm forced to use all the power within me."

He digested this before nodding. "I'm sorry. I didn't realize what I was asking of you. I just knew that I would do whatever it took to spare my son. Hamish must have been much nearer death than I'd thought, if it took all your power to bring him back."

She didn't know what caught her more by surprise—his apology, or his unquestioning acceptance of her explanation. "You believe me?"

"After seeing what you did for my son, I'm willing to believe anything. Whether you are witch or wizard, I care not, my lady."

"I am no witch, my lord. I am merely a woman who has learned to use certain powers that are within all of us."

A mere woman? He doubted that. Still, there was no denying the way his body was responding to the nearness of her. If she were any other woman, he might be willing to give in to the need to pleasure himself and her. He had to keep reminding himself that she could ensnare him, and he would be powerless to stop her.

"If that be so, why doesn't everyone possess such powers?"

"My grandmother said it's because people have forgotten."

That had him smiling. "And how have you remembered?"

She tried to ignore his smile, though it wasn't easy. She much preferred his frown. At least then she could remember that he was the lout who had brought her here against her will. When he smiled like this she felt something twist and turn deep inside her.

"I learned from my mother. And she learned from hers. Perhaps those without mothers were the first to forget."

She saw his smile fade and remembered, too late, the woman hovering around young Hamish's bedside.

Her voice fell. "Others simply got careless. Or ashamed of the powers they possessed. According to my mother, those who had lost their power began to persecute those who still had it."

"So that's why you live in the Mystical Kingdom? To avoid persecution?"

"Life is simpler there. We accept what we have without question or regret."

"Are there others like you living there?"

She shook her head. "Only my family, and Bessie and Jeremy."

"You have no men there other than that troll?"

Her eyes flashed a fiery challenge. "What need have we of men? What can they possibly do for us that we can't do for ourselves?"

"They can protect you. And catch game for your food. And build you fine cottages."

"We protect ourselves, my lord, though the only danger comes from outside our kingdom. As for food and shelter, we provide our own."

"I saw your garden. And I also saw how much

work you put into it to till the soil and raise the crops.''

''I don't mind hard work. Nor do the other women in my family. You see? We do very well on our own. We've no need of men.''

''Aye. I do see. It would appear that your mother hasn't told you everything.''

She saw something come into his eyes. Something dark and knowing that had her puzzled. ''I don't understand.''

''Men can be good for other things.'' He lowered his head until his mouth hovered over hers. ''Like this.''

His lips whispered over hers as gently as the wings of a butterfly. He saw her eyes widen with stunned surprise, unaware that his own reaction had been similar.

He'd meant only to tease her. But he was the one being teased. One sweet taste and he knew he wanted more.

Before she could push away he gathered her firmly against him and took the kiss deeper.

What exotic flavors were here. A sweetness he wanted to explore at greater length. She tasted of summer sun. Hot. Sizzling. And of rainwater, pure and clear and fresh. He'd never known a woman's lips to be so soft. So perfect.

He hadn't planned this. But now that his mouth

was on hers, there was no turning back. He was completely lost in the enticing taste of her.

As for Allegra, she couldn't think. Couldn't form even one coherent thought. All she could do was curl her fingers into the hair at his chest and hold on as the room seemed to dip and spin in lazy circles.

Why was her heart racing so? What had happened to her will? Why was she content to lie here in this man's arms and allow him to take such liberties?

Lost in his kiss, she sighed. She'd never known a man's lips could be so clever. With just the slightest movement on hers, they caused her blood to heat and her bones to melt. She could feel her pulse racing, and wondered that her poor heart could continue to keep up such a heady pace without simply bursting from the effort.

When he continued to kiss her until she was breathless, she let out a whimper. In reply he moaned and took the kiss deeper still, until both their hearts were thundering.

Slowly, ever so slowly he found the strength to lift his head, breaking contact.

"What have you done to me?" He stared down at her as though thunderstruck, and was reminded of his cousin's warning. "Woman, you've bewitched me."

Tossing aside the furs, he swung away from her and got unsteadily to his feet.

At the door he paused. "I'll have Mistress MacDonald send a servant with a meal for you and the lad."

"And a horse," Allegra shouted back when she managed to find her voice. "For I've done your bidding, and now you must keep your promise and return me to my family."

"I've told you I'm a man of my word. A horse will be made ready." He turned and strode down the hall, furious with himself for forgetting, for even one minute, how dangerous this woman was. Even now, with distance between them, he wanted her. His hands were trembling. He clutched them firmly at his sides as he stormed away.

If he allowed her to entice him, she would soon use her powers to control him. It was absolutely essential that he summon the strength to resist.

Still, it was easier to tell his mind than his body. With but a single kiss, he'd been completely aroused. There was something so innocent, so sweet about Allegra Drummond. If he didn't know better, he'd swear she'd never been with a man. And he'd wanted, more than anything else, to be her first. He'd wanted, in those few moments, to fill himself with all that goodness, that innocence. To take and give until they were both sated.

But how could he know if she was truly a maiden, or if this was all a clever plan on her part to entrap him?

It was magic, pure and simple, and he'd be well rid of her this day.

With his mind in turmoil, he snarled at a servant, bellowed at poor Mistress MacDonald and soon had the entire household scurrying about, eager to see to the lord's needs.

In Hamish's chambers, Allegra paced in front of the fire, trying to figure out what had just happened. One minute Merrick MacAndrew was kissing her until she was dizzy. The next he was storming out of the chambers accusing her of bewitching him.

In truth, she was the one who'd been bewitched. By a surly, headstrong warrior. These strange feelings he'd awakened in her had her trembling with fear. She'd never known a man's touch, his kiss, could affect her in such a manner.

For those few moments he'd had a power over her that had left her own powers diminished to the point that she was helpless. It wasn't a feeling she liked.

And yet… She touched a fingertip to her lips. Even now she could taste him. Could feel the tingling where he'd touched her. Could feel the strange liquid warmth deep within. What was this power? What was it called?

He was a strange one. He'd brought her here against her will. Had bullied her, called her witch and watched her as one might watch a villain. Yet this same man had spent the night in her bed, warming her with his own body, bringing her back, by sheer determination, from the very brink of darkness.

She was grateful to him, of course. But now they were even, for she'd spent herself bringing his son back from the brink, as well.

His son. She turned away from the fire and knelt beside the lad's pallet. His color was good, his breathing normal. She was about to turn away when she sensed something disturbing. She touched her fingertips to his temples and went very still. In his mind was great torment. She could sense murky, whirling clouds that obliterated the light.

Something had happened to the lad. Some conflict that left him terribly afraid. Whatever it was, it had not yet been resolved. And until it was, the darkness would continue to cloud his mind.

She got to her feet and, crossing her arms over her chest, became lost in thought. The lad's demons were not her problem. With the love of all these people around him, he would find resolution, given enough time. Besides, she was a healer, not a reader of minds.

She had done what his father had demanded. She had brought the lad back from the brink. Now without further delay she must return to the safety of the Mystical Kingdom, and the love of her family. Especially in light of that kiss. She needed to escape Merrick MacAndrew and his strange power.

"I've brought biscuits and ale." Mistress MacDonald hurried into the chambers, and directed a serving wench who carried a tray.

Allegra whirled to face them, then managed to compose herself. "Thank you, Mistress MacDonald."

As the tray of food was uncovered the old woman turned. "How did our lad sleep last night?"

Allegra nodded toward the figure in the nest of furs. "He slept well, as you can see."

"Aye." The housekeeper's face softened into a beatific smile. "The household buzzes with happiness at our lord's good fortune, especially since both father and son have suffered so much pain."

"Pain?" Allegra arched a brow.

"Of course. Ye wouldn't have heard." The old woman was quick to dismiss the servant. When the door was closed she lowered her voice. "The lad's mother was found dead, after falling from her balcony."

"How could such a thing happen?"

The housekeeper clutched her hands together. "There's no explanation for it." Her voice sank. "At least, none that is acceptable." The old woman's head lifted in an unusual act of defiance for one so humble. "I know what others think. That the lord caused this unspeakable thing."

"But why?"

The old woman shrugged. "Some say when he became weary of his wife's strange behavior and threatened to lock her away for her own good, she chose to end her life rather than submit. Others whisper that he simply was pushed to the limit of his patience and took matters into his own hands."

Allegra's hand went to her throat. Such a thing was unthinkable in her enchanted land. But she had heard tales from her mother and grandmother, of the dark spirits that roamed the earth, enticing mortals to embrace their evil. "Do you believe such a thing, Mistress MacDonald?"

The old woman shook her head. "I know what others call him. The Sword of the Highlands. A cruel, hardened warrior. But it wasn't always so. When he was a lad like Hamish, he was kind and loving. But he changed. Both he and his wife changed."

"In what way?"

Again that shrug of shoulder. "The lady became...odd. Some said she was mad. She often roamed the castle at night, or the gardens, as though driven by demons.''

"What of young Hamish?'' Allegra glanced over at the sleeping lad. "How was he affected by all this?''

"We'd believed him to be fine, at first. But I see him changing, as well. With his father often away at war, there have been...spells.''

"Spells?''

The old woman lowered her voice. "Times when the lad seems to slip away from us. He seems to go somewhere in his mind, and then he has no recollection of things he's said or done.'' She began wringing her hands. "Lady Catherine's death left both the lord and his son alone. For more than a year now, the lord has been away, fighting one battle after another. And though his countrymen are grateful, those of us here in Berkshire Castle can see what his absence is doing to the lad. Not that we blame the lord, ye understand. For he must see to the safety of all his people. And perhaps he chooses to stay away because when he returns and looks at Hamish, he sees his beloved Catherine. That's reason enough for a man to put distance between himself and the one who causes him pain, until he can find some sort of peace.''

"Do you really believe the lord can ever find peace if he caused the death of his own wife?"

"That's not for me to know." The old woman straightened her shoulders, aware that she'd given away far too much to this stranger. But it was easy to talk to this witch. To tell her things so long kept inside. Now it was time to be sensible. "I've had ye'r gown cleaned, in preparation for ye'r journey home." She gave Allegra a long look. "The servants are whispering about it, for it's finer than anything they've ever seen."

"My mother works the loom, weaves the cloth and sews the gowns my sisters and I wear. She learned from her mother, whose work was once commissioned by royalty."

"'Tis no wonder it's so grand." Mistress MacDonald turned away. "Ye're to summon a servant as soon as our lad wakes. The lord has ordered his most trusted warriors to escort ye back to ye'r home."

"Thank you, Mistress."

When the old woman was gone, Allegra ignored the food and resumed her pacing, her mind in sudden turmoil.

The tale of mysterious death had touched her deeply. Hadn't she sensed the darkness when she'd first set foot in Berkshire Castle? She had no way of knowing if the lord had been involved in it, for it was impossible to see into his heart. But what of the lad? She paused to study him. He was so young. So sweet. And without a mother in whom he could confide.

Allegra tried to imagine her life without her mother and grandmother. Such strong, wise women. There was nothing she couldn't tell them. She knew her family was grieving the loss of her, as she was missing them. She could feel it in her soul. She yearned to be with them. And if she said nothing more about the lad's troubles, she could be back in the Mystical Kingdom by this time on the morrow.

Of course, if she were to leave now, the lad would have to deal with his demons on his own, for he had only a father now. A father who had been absent for much of his young life. Still, Merrick MacAndrew was strong and capable. A seasoned warrior who knew everything there was to know about fighting his enemy on the field of battle. A fair man who had stayed with her through the night, bringing her back from the Valley of Mist. Even now he was preparing to keep his word and return her to her home.

But could he deal with a little boy's inner demons? Was he equipped to teach his son how to face down the terrors that came in the night?

Perhaps, if she hadn't heard about his mother's fate, she wouldn't now be suffering such anxiety about leaving Hamish alone with his problems.

She pressed her fingertips to her own temples, hoping to calm the turmoil within. Why did she have to care so deeply about others? It had always been her greatest weakness. And it always ended up causing her such conflict.

After more pacing she gave a sigh of resignation and removed the night shift. Slipping into her gown, she began preparing for the journey home.

Chapter Six

"Here ye are, lad." Mistress MacDonald bustled about the chambers, directing a serving wench. "I was given orders by the lord himself that ye were to eat sufficient to gain back ye'r strength. Mara has brought you gruel laced with honey."

As the young servant placed the bowl on the table, the old woman hovered over the boy's pallet. "Are ye strong enough to sit at the table?"

"I think so." As Hamish leaned on the old woman's arm and crossed to the table, he glanced at Allegra, who stood across the room. "Who is the beautiful lady?"

"The healer."

"Healer?" His eyes rounded as he made his way slowly to the table. "Have you a name?"

"Allegra Drummond." She walked close and offered him a smile.

"Allegra." He thought a minute. "That means joyful. Are you filled with joy?"

"I suppose I am. At least most of the time. How is it you know the meaning of my name?"

"My mother taught me the meanings of many names. She said mine meant heavenly gift." When he was seated, he indicated the chair across from him.

Allegra sat and accepted a goblet of hot mulled wine from the servant. "You're fortunate to have had such a wise woman for a mother."

"Was your mother wise?"

"She is."

"She's still alive?" He helped himself to a bite of gruel, eating slowly, like one who had forgotten how, and wiped his mouth with his sleeve. "Does she tell you stories and sing to you until you fall asleep?"

"She did when I was younger."

He thought about that a moment, then said casually, "Father said I fell from a tree."

Allegra nodded, delighting in the way his mind seemed to leap from one thought to another. Perhaps she had worried in vain. The lad seemed bright and strong and cheerful.

"How old are you, Hamish?"

"Five." He glanced at the housekeeper. "Or am I six?"

"Ye're still five, lad."

He turned to Allegra. "Why did I need a healer?"

"You were hurt. You fell into a deep sleep, and those who love you feared that you might not wake without my help."

He paused and blinked, remembering just for a fleeting moment that face, and that soft, musical voice, breaking through the darkness that had surrounded him. Then the image was gone. His mind became a blank canvas.

He ate in silence before looking up at the housekeeper. "Is Father truly home, Mistress MacDonald? Or was that only a dream?"

"'Twas no dream, lad. The lord seems truly glad to be home with ye."

Hamish ducked his head, but not before Allegra caught sight of the smile of happiness that lit his eyes. He ate several bites of gruel before pushing the bowl away.

The housekeeper clucked like a mother hen. "That's not enough to keep a bird alive, lad."

"I'll try again later, Mistress MacDonald."

Allegra drained her wine and looked up when Merrick MacAndrew came hurrying into the room, trailed by his cousins.

"Mordred and Desmond have offered to return you to your home."

Allegra felt a chill pass over her. She glanced at

the balcony, wondering if a storm threatened. Seeing no clouds, she turned back. "I thank you, my lord. But why do you not send a company of warriors?"

Mordred's tone was haughty. "My brother and I need no warriors."

She tried a smile, though it was strained. "You're to be commended. There aren't many men who would consent to travel to the Mystical Kingdom without benefit of an army."

Mordred gave a short huff of breath. "Our cousin did so, and seemed none the worse for it. Besides, Merrick has assured us that he already slew the dragon that stands guard at the banks of the Enchanted Loch."

Allegra couldn't help asking, "What makes you think there was only one dragon?"

She saw Mordred's self-assured smile fade.

Merrick gave her a measured look. "Will you give me your word that my cousins will not be mistreated when they arrive at your kingdom? There will be no sudden storms? No monsters rising up out of the loch?"

"I can assure you that once I arrive at my home safely, my family will be there to greet me. They'll see my escorts rewarded with a feast before sending them on their way."

Merrick drew a quiet breath. "That eases my

mind considerably.'' He brightened as he looked at
his son. ''I see you've eaten, Hamish.''

''Aye, Father.''

Merrick turned back to Allegra. ''He seems fully
recovered from his injury.''

Allegra ignored the tiny ripple of disquiet. ''We
had a grand visit while he ate. The lad has a quick
mind.''

''So I'm told.'' That brought a smile to his lips
as he handed Allegra a hooded cloak. ''This was my
wife's. I asked Mistress MacDonald to fetch it for
your journey home.''

''Thank you. That was most generous of you, my
lord.'' As Allegra accepted it, their fingers brushed.

The jolt of heat was like a lightning bolt that had
them both pulling back. Merrick wondered whether
there had been sparks, or if it had been his imagi-
nation. Whatever had just happened, it had him
more uneasy than he cared to admit. His fingers
were still tingling from the contact.

Allegra turned away, her hands trembling as she
slipped into the cloak and tucked her hair beneath
the hood.

When she turned back, she had her features composed. She wouldn't let herself dwell on this strange
magic that Merrick MacAndrew possessed. Instead
she would think about the journey home.

Oh, Mama. The danger is behind me now. Tell

Gram and Kylia and Gwenellen that by this time on the morrow, I'll be with them.

Merrick bowed before her, careful not to touch her again. "I thank you, Allegra Drummond, for healing my son. And now I wish you safe journey."

"And I thank you, Merrick MacAndrew, for keeping your word to me. May you and Hamish stay well."

At the mention of his name the little boy called out to her, "Healer, am I allowed to walk in the gardens?"

She smiled. "I don't see why not. Though I do think you should stay close to the keep until you're a bit stronger. And perhaps you should lean on a servant, at least for today."

"I will." He pushed away from the table and laughed when Mistress MacDonald offered her arm. "Are you going to walk with me?"

The old woman was beaming. "I've been waiting for this day, lad. There's no chore that could be more important than spending an hour with my young Hamish in the garden."

Before they could take their leave, the old woman paused to press a gnarled hand over Allegra's. Though she was still frightened of this witch, making her words awkward and halting, they needed to be said. "Bless ye, my lady. Ye've brought the sunshine back into all our lives." As she started away she called, "Safe journey, my lady."

"Thank you, Mistress MacDonald." Allegra watched as the old woman and little boy disappeared down the hall.

As she walked from the room, flanked by Mordred and Desmond, a chill passed through her, and she had to struggle to push it aside. She was aware of Merrick keeping pace behind her, but she kept her head high, her gaze fixed on the door that led to the courtyard.

Once outside she walked to the horse, being held by a groom. Before she could pull herself into the saddle Mordred was there, ready to assist her.

The moment his hands circled her waist she felt an icy chill that had her trembling violently. As she accepted the reins from the groom, she had to struggle to compose herself.

Merrick stepped close, careful not to touch her. Seeing her pallor, he asked, "What is it, my lady? Are you ill?"

"Nay." She forced the fear aside, reminding herself that she would soon be back with her family. "Just a chill."

He stepped back. "I bid you safe journey, then." He turned and shaded the sun from his eyes. "And you, my cousins."

Mordred gave him an easy smile before saluting

and starting off at a brisk trot. Desmond, stone-faced, waited for Allegra to make her move.

Allegra wheeled her mount to follow. Just then she heard a woman's scream.

"M'lord!" Mistress MacDonald was wailing like a banshee. "Ye must come at once."

"Hold." Merrick reached out and caught the bridle of Allegra's mount. "You'll not leave until we see what's happened."

Before she could issue a protest he'd hauled her roughly from the saddle and closed a hand around her wrist, dragging her along as he followed the entire household toward the garden.

As they hurried along the ancient stone walkway, they saw the lad lying in the grass, his body twisting and writhing.

The old woman stood over him, wringing her hands. She looked up, eyes wide with terror. "Oh, sweet heaven, m'lord. It's Hamish. Come quick. The lad's possessed."

The servants quickly fell back in fear. As Merrick strode forward, with Allegra beside him, many of the servants began muttering among themselves.

"'Tis the work of the witch."

"Or the work of the devil."

"They're one and the same. And now she's turned the poor lad into one, as well."

"He'd have been better off dead. Now he'll end up just like his poor mother."

That had many of them nodding in agreement.

Allegra ignored the comments as she stood watching Merrick, who knelt beside his son and gathered him into his arms.

"Hush now, Hamish, lad. I'm here. Tell me what's wrong."

The boy continued to twitch and moan, as though in unbearable pain.

Frantic, Merrick looked up at Allegra. His voice was gruff with fear and accusation. "You said he was healed."

"I did as you asked, and brought him out of his sleep."

"That isn't enough." His fingers snagged her wrist and he dragged her roughly to her knees beside him, leaving the crowd of onlookers gasping.

Through gritted teeth he snarled, "You'll find out what's wrong with my son, woman, and make it right."

Allegra felt the sting of humiliation as the crowd closed in, suddenly eager to see her work her magic. She had a flash of memory, and was back in her childhood, hearing the muttering of an angry crowd when she had innocently saved a lad from drowning.

She lifted her head. "You'll first send the others away."

"You dare to order me...?" Though Merrick's eyes flashed with fury, he was in no position to argue. He turned to his housekeeper. "Mistress MacDonald. You'll see that the servants are taken inside." He looked up at his cousins, who hovered over them, looking both angry and confused. "I'll not need you today. I'll send word when the woman is ready to leave."

Allegra ignored the harshness of his tone. For now, her only thoughts must be for the lad.

Mordred crossed his arms over his chest. "I think it best that we stay."

Following his brother's lead, Desmond nodded.

"Nay." Merrick shook his head. "You'll go. Now. I command it."

Mordred seemed about to protest when he caught the icy look in his cousin's eyes. With a last glance at the woman, he turned and led Desmond back to the castle.

When they were alone Allegra tossed aside the cloak and touched her fingertips to Hamish's temples. At once the violent twitching faded until he lay as still as death.

Allegra closed her eyes and concentrated.

She frowned, struggling to find a way through the whirling mist that clouded his mind. "There is much darkness here."

"What causes the darkness?" Merrick knelt beside her. "Is it fear? Anger?"

"Fear, I believe, though it is mingled with many other emotions. Anger." She concentrated a moment before adding, "Shame."

"Shame? What does my son have to be ashamed of?"

She shook her head and struggled to focus. "I'm not certain, but I believe it shamed him to run from this fear. There is guilt because he didn't stay and face it as a warrior might have."

"He's just a lad." Merrick caught his son's hand in his. So small. So helpless. "What does he know about being a warrior?"

Her eyes opened and she turned to the man beside her. "When you look at him, you see his mother's face. But he is his father's son, as well. It is you he admires above all else. It is you he wants to imitate."

She saw his jaw tighten. His words were forced, angry. "I know I gave my word that I would return you to your home if you brought him back to me. If you insist on leaving, I will have no choice but to keep my word. But I would ask a favor of you." His voice lowered with feeling, for it galled him to beg. "I would be most grateful if you would stay and help my son remember his fear, so that he can face it and move on with his life."

Allegra knew what it cost this proud man to ask such a thing. As lord, he could order it, and she would have no choice but to obey. After all, no matter what he chose to call her, she was his captive. There was no one here in Berkshire Castle, or in the village beyond, who would assist her without the lord's approval.

"What if, by helping Hamish remember his fear, it should cause him peril?"

"He and I will face whatever peril it might bring together. I want my son back. Well and whole again."

She caught a glimpse of movement beyond him and watched as a shimmering light seemed to transform itself into the lovely, golden-haired woman she'd first seen in Hamish's mind. The woman was holding out her hands as though imploring Allegra to stay.

When Allegra blinked, the image was gone.

What things had transpired here, to cause the woman to linger long past her time? What strange matter was unfinished here, and begging for a resolution?

Allegra paused for long, silent moments before nodding. "As much as I yearn for my home in the Mystical Kingdom, I can't leave the lad alone and helpless against these unknown fears, without doing all in my power to help him." She took in a deep breath. "I'm not certain I can find a way through the maze that fills his mind, for as I've told you, that isn't my gift. My only gift is healing. But I give you my word that I will try."

Merrick studied her eyes. They were wise beyond her years. And filled with compassion.

He had a sudden thought. "Will you be forced to pay the same price as before?"

She nodded. "There is no denying that it will exact a price of me. Each time I use my gift, I must pay. This will surely weaken me, but not drain me as before. The journey from the other side is the greatest, and demands the most. Much more so than the journey from past to present."

He nodded in understanding. "I'll see that the chamber beside Hamish's is prepared for you. You're to let Mistress MacDonald know what you need. Whether it is food or rest or herbs that you require, all will be provided."

He lifted the now quiet boy into his arms and started toward the house, with Allegra following. She looked up to see the housekeeper and servants peering anxiously from doorways and balcony windows.

What had she just agreed to? Though she was not to blame for what had happened to the lad, there were many here who would be quick to blame her if Hamish should suffer any ill effects. They would be watching and waiting to see if she were truly a witch. Even those things outside her realm— weather, plague, the cruelty of others—would somehow be blamed on her.

She had once again, it would seem, put herself in harm's way for someone she barely knew. And all because of her foolish, tender heart.

Would she never learn?

Chapter Seven

As they entered the keep, Merrick began shouting orders, sending the servants scattering to do his bidding.

Allegra followed Merrick into his son's chambers, watching as Hamish was tucked beneath a blanket of fur. Using the last of the herbs, she quickly ground the leaves and added them to a goblet of hot water. When the tea had steeped she held it to the lad's lips and helped him drink.

Satisfied, she set the goblet aside. "For now, my lord, I think the lad should be allowed to sleep. He has been on a long and harrowing journey, and both his body and mind are still weary."

Merrick dropped to his knees and took the boy's hand in his, staring down at the face, now peaceful in rest. "It tears at my heart to see him so tormented."

"Aye." Allegra dropped to her knees on the other side of the pallet and smoothed the covers. "But sleep is healing. To the mind as well as the body. I suspect that when he awakens, he'll have no memory of this latest incident in the garden."

"If he doesn't remember, how can you help him?"

"We all have memories that we've forgotten, my lord. But deep inside, our minds retain them. And sometimes when we least expect it, the memory bubbles to the surface. I must first gain Hamish's trust. And then perhaps I can find a way through the mists to the thing that troubles him."

"M'lord." The housekeeper paused in the doorway, glancing nervously from Merrick to the young woman who had everyone in the fortress feeling so uneasy. "As you requested, the lady's chambers have been prepared for her."

"Thank you, Mistress MacDonald." Merrick turned to Allegra. "What do you require?"

She glanced at the traveling cloak, which she'd tossed on a nearby chaise. This day was to have been her joyous return to her home. And now, once again, her plans were thwarted.

"I must send a missive to my family, assuring them that I am well and that I am no longer being held against my will. Will you order one of your men to deliver it?"

For the first time since their encounter that morning, he smiled, and she realized with a jolt how dangerously handsome the lord of Berkshire Castle was. "Why can you not simply ease your family's worries with a thought?"

"Such a thing is possible during times of extreme danger. I know that my family sensed your presence in our kingdom and gathered together to guard against your strength."

"The storm that tossed the waters?" His eyes narrowed. "They sent it?"

"Aye. And could have done more, but they feared they would harm me, as well as you. The fact that you refused to release me diminished their powers."

"A lucky happenstance." He nodded. "All right, my lady. Write your missive and I'll have one of my men deliver it to your home."

"He need not risk his life by crossing the Enchanted Loch. If he but places it in a pouch made of kidskin, it will drift across the loch to the opposite shore, where my family will find it."

Merrick's smile widened. "So many secrets. Does this mean you're beginning to trust me?"

"As much as you trust me, my lord."

That had him throwing back his head and roaring with laughter. "By heaven, you are a clever woman, the likes of which I've never known."

"And you're a harsh man. But I think a fair one."

She stood and brushed down her skirts. "I'll need parchment and a quill. My family has worried long enough."

He looked at the housekeeper, hovering in the doorway, and the surly young serving wench, Mara, beside her. "See to whatever the lady requires, Mistress."

When the old woman had given orders to the servant, Allegra glanced over at Merrick. He was studying her with a look that had the color rushing to her cheeks. Despite the distance between them, she could feel his touch as surely as though he'd reached out to her. Could almost taste his lips on hers.

More of his magic, she thought as she followed the housekeeper to her chambers. The man had such strange powers.

Merrick remained beside his son's pallet, listening to the swish of Allegra's skirts until she was gone. If he were honest, he would have to admit that out there in the courtyard he'd had a moment of regret about her leaving. And then, in a blink, almost as if his wish were being granted, there'd been a compelling reason for her to stay.

He would have to remain vigilant. For there was something about this witch that touched a chord in him. It would be so easy to fool himself into believing that she was merely sweet and innocent and good. But then, any woman with such potent magic as hers could persuade a man to believe anything. He'd soon be believing that witches had no interest in seducing mortal men, though everyone knew they did.

He had no intention of falling victim to her charms.

His only concern must be Hamish. He would not rest until the lad was whole and well and happy once more.

He fervently hoped this woman's healing reached the mind as well as the body, for the lad's condition was deeply troubling. In the deepest, darkest recesses of his mind he harbored the terrible fear that Hamish was following his mother into madness.

Allegra tiptoed into the lad's chambers and knelt beside his pallet, listening to the soft, steady sound of his breathing. Assured that his sleep was untroubled, she got to her feet and shook down her skirts. In the morning she intended to walk to the nearby field and forest and begin gathering the plants and herbs she would need for healing.

In the hallway candles sputtering in puddles of melted wax cast eerie shadows across the walls.

As she was about to pass the staircase Allegra paused in midstride. It wasn't so much a sound as a feeling that had her looking over her shoulder. A prickly feeling that someone was following her. The next thing she knew she'd been shoved roughly from behind. With a cry of alarm she found herself toppling headfirst down the stairs.

For a moment she lay on the hard wooden floor, feeling the room spinning in dizzying circles. As her head cleared she gingerly touched a hand to her head and felt the beginnings of a lump. She sat up and looked around, but there was no sign of anyone around.

She sat for several more minutes until she was certain she could stand. With a quiet sigh of resignation she got to her feet and made her way up the stairs and to her room.

As she climbed into bed she knew, without a doubt, that her fall had been no accident. Someone was making it very clear that she wasn't wanted here at Berkshire Castle.

This deliberate act of cruelty only firmed her resolve to stay and watch out for the lad. For there was much more here than she'd first anticipated.

''What is this?'' Allegra glanced up when Mistress MacDonald entered her chamber, followed by a parade of serving wenches. One carried an empty tub deep enough to sit in. After setting it on several layers of linen, she departed, while several more women emptied buckets of steaming water until the tub was filled. All looked around quickly, as though in mortal danger, and seemed eager to depart the witch's chambers.

The frowning young serving wench who usually attended Hamish entered Allegra's chambers, bearing an armload of gowns and assorted feminine frills.

The housekeeper looked around uneasily at the bundles of herbs that Allegra had picked in the garden and nearby field. So many of them. The room was perfumed with their fragrance. "The lord has ordered me to see that these gowns are made to fit ye. Mara is a lazy, surly wench, but is also an accomplished seamstress. She'll see to ye'r needs."

Allegra couldn't hide her impatience as she began hanging the herbs to dry. "I am merely a healer. What need have I of fine gowns?"

The old woman was already laying out the items across the bedcovers. "The lord has commanded that ye join him in the great hall to sup."

"I see." Allegra gave a disinterested glance at the array of gowns and shawls, petticoats and kid slippers, then returned her attention to her plants. "You may choose for me, Mistress MacDonald. As for me, I must prepare a balm for the lad."

While she busied herself crushing the leaves of several herbs in a bowl, the housekeeper picked up a lovely gown the color of heather.

"This will do, Mara. I believe it will suit the lady. If it is too big, use one of these ribbons to cinch the waist." She handed over a shawl of soft ivory, threaded with heather ribbons. "And this, I believe to chase the chill of the great room."

Mistress MacDonald saw the way the servant was eyeing the concoction in Allegra's bowl. She understood the fear and loathing, for it was there in her own mind, as well. But the lord had decided to trust this healer, and from what the old woman had seen, Allegra Drummond seemed genuinely interested in healing the lad.

She took the servant's arm and shook her. "Listen to me, Mara. Ye will see to the lady's every need, or the lord will have ye'r head. Do ye understand?"

The servant gave a defiant toss of her head. "Aye, Mistress MacDonald."

"Good. And dress the lady's hair, if that be possible." The old woman gave a dubious look at the wild mane of fiery tresses that spilled down Allegra's back. It would take more skill than Mara possessed to tame that unsightly tangle. Still, she knew the servant would do what she'd been told. And anything would be better than the way the healer looked now, like some wild creature just dragged in from a Highland forest.

Mistress MacDonald flounced from the room, her

mind awhirl with the dozens of chores requiring her attention.

When Allegra had finished with her herbs, she glanced at the servant, studying her so carefully. "Where shall we begin, Mara?"

"A proper bath, if you please, my lady."

"Aye. I think that can be arranged." Removing her gown, Allegra settled herself into the warm water and sank down with a sigh of pure pleasure.

"I was given orders to wash your hair, my lady." Mara stood several paces away, looking her over with disdain.

"Well, then." Allegra struggled to hold back the uneasy tingle along her spine. Was this to be her reaction to all she met in this castle? "We wouldn't want you to disobey an order, would we?" She deliberately closed her eyes and sank down into the water, soaking her hair before coming up for air. "You may begin washing, Mara."

The servant worked up a lather and began scrubbing Allegra's hair, carefully parting it as she did.

Allegra couldn't resist saying, "Have you found them yet?"

"Found what?"

"The horns."

The girl's hands stilled and she jerked back. "H-horns, my lady?"

"Isn't that what you were looking for, Mara?"

"Aye."

Allegra's laugh bubbled out, clear as a bell. "You need have no fear. There are no horns. Nor wings, I fear. I am neither saint nor sinner, but just a woman, the same as you."

"The same as I?" The serving wench remained unconvinced. With a trace of annoyance she said, "Would you mind rinsing, my lady?"

Allegra sank beneath the water, shaking her hair until it was rinsed clean. As she stepped from the tub she could see the servant looking her over. It would seem that no amount of assurance would ease the girl's mind until she saw for herself that the healer was, indeed, a mere woman.

Allegra stood in front of the fireplace while the servant helped her into a chemise and petticoats, stockings and kid slippers, and then into the gown. When she was dressed she sat on a low bench to allow the servant to brush her hair. It seemed an hour before Mara was satisfied.

Finally she led Allegra to a tall looking glass. "Here you are, my lady."

Allegra was caught by surprise. Except for her reflection in the Enchanted Loch, she'd never seen herself as others saw her. Certainly not with such clarity.

She ran her hands down the skirt, then raised them to pat her hair. "Are you a witch, Mara?"

"My lady?"

Allegra gave a lilting laugh. "Surely you have magic in your hands. How else do you explain how you have turned a turnip into a rose?"

The girl's eyes narrowed with suspicion. "What a strange thing to say. Have you never before seen your own beauty?"

Allegra turned away. "I've no interest in how I look. My mother told me that the only thing that matters is what's in our hearts." She snatched up the bowl of crushed herbs. "Now I must go. I've wasted enough time on my own pleasures. It's time to see how Hamish is faring."

The servant reached for the bowl. "I can take that to him, my lady."

Allegra paused. "Nay. I'll see to it myself."

With a scowl Mara draped the shawl around her shoulders as she started toward the door. "You'd best not tarry. The lord sups at dusk."

"I'll be there." Allegra paused in the doorway. "I thank you, Mara."

The servant looked stunned by her gratitude. Never before had anyone thanked her for doing her duty.

When the lady was gone the young servant picked up Allegra's discarded gown and studied the golden threads, the fine, even stitches. Such fabric. As soft, as delicate as though spun by angels.

Or witches.

The thought had her going very still. She'd expected someone very different from the simple, friendly lass who displayed equal parts of wit and charm. But she would do well to remember that the lady she served was not like others. She would be clever and sly and quick of mind.

But then, she wasn't the only one.

"So, Merrick. You survived the Mystical Kingdom." A cluster of warriors stood by the fire, enjoying their ale.

"Aye." Merrick glanced idly over the crowd that had begun gathering in the great room.

"Was it as we'd heard? Are there monsters in the loch, and wicked mists that can blind a man?"

"I saw no mists. But there was a dragon. And a dozen or more warriors."

"Are you saying, without benefit of companions you slew a dragon as well as a dozen armed men?"

"I had no thought of my own safety. It was for Hamish. And, as you can see, I'm still standing." He noted the number of women from the village, many of whom he hadn't seen since burying his wife. "I see you've brought your ladies tonight."

"Your cousins assured us it would be all right. Our women didn't want to miss the chance to see a real witch," one of the men said with a laugh.

Merrick frowned into his goblet. "I trust you'll refrain from calling her that, Malcolm."

The man ignored the thread of anger. "I hear she brought Hamish out of his sleep."

"Aye."

"And now he's possessed."

Merrick felt a sense of growing agitation. "He merely fell in the garden."

"We heard that he took a fit."

"The lad is still weak and…" Merrick's voice trailed off when he caught sight of Allegra standing in the doorway. For a moment all he could see was the proud lift of her head as she surveyed the crowd. Her hair had been dressed with ribbons and pulled to one side, spilling over her breast. Her gown, the color of heather, seemed to add a pretty blush to her cheeks.

Standing beside her was Hamish, looking absolutely terrified as he held firmly to her hand.

Mordred followed the direction of Merrick's gaze and sneered. "Has the witch snatched your voice, cousin?"

Merrick ignored his cousin's taunts and crossed the room in quick strides, scooping his son into his arms. "Are you feeling strong enough to sup, lad?"

"Aye, Father. The healer told me I've been sleeping most of the day. Now I'm feeling rested."

"I'm glad, Hamish." Merrick brushed a kiss on

his son's cheek before turning to Allegra. "I see Mistress MacDonald found something for you to wear."

"Aye. My compliments. It was a most clever plan."

"A clever plan?" His smile evaporated. "I fear I don't understand."

Allegra surveyed the women, whispering behind their hands, and the men, staring at her with open curiosity. "I see now why you insisted that I join you in the great room, my lord."

"You do?"

"Aye. I should have realized what you had in mind." She lifted her head higher, and straightened her spine. "I can see by the eager looks on your guests' faces that I'm to be the evening's entertainment."

Chapter Eight

Merrick's puzzled frown became a scowl. "Woman, you're mistaken. It's not as it appears…" Before he could finish, his housekeeper rushed up to announce in a breathless voice that everyone should take their places at table so the wenches could commence serving.

"I know how ye insist upon supping exactly at dusk, m'lord." Seeing him in the doorway, the old woman flashed him a brilliant smile. "Are ye not pleased to see the lad up and about?"

Merrick swallowed back his hiss of frustration at the old woman's untimely arrival. He certainly didn't owe the healer an explanation. "Aye, Mistress MacDonald."

"Well, then, m'lord, if ye'll take the seat of honor, we'll begin the meal." The housekeeper added, with a trace of pride, "I think ye'll agree that

Cook has outdone herself tonight, in honor of the lad's return to us from his sleep.''

As Merrick led his son between the tables, he could hear the whispers and muffled laughter, aimed at the woman who trailed behind. There was an almost palpable sense of fear and excitement rippling through the crowd.

''Do you think she'll cast a spell?''

''Perhaps she'll turn you into a toad, Duncan.''

That elicited much laughter.

Two village women, known for their love of gossip, giggled behind their hands.

''She doesn't look like a witch.''

''What does a witch look like? Have you ever seen one, Lissa?''

''Nay. But she moves like a witch. See? Without any effort. As though floating.''

''Aye. And look at her hands, the fingers long and tapered. With but a snap of those fingers, she can conjure images, dark and frightening.''

''And why not? Witches are in league with the devil.''

Merrick understood their mutterings, for wasn't he guilty of the same foolish fears? But so many of his notions had been vanquished once he'd met the woman beneath the myth. Still, it galled him to know that she was subjected to such cruel treatment from his own people. Whether driven by fear or ignorance, they had to understand that their words were hurtful to the one who heard them.

When he reached the head table, Mordred and Desmond were already waiting. Though they greeted Hamish with enthusiasm, they were restrained in their approach to the woman. It would seem that they, too, had their reservations about her.

Instead of taking his place at table, Merrick motioned for silence. At once the room fell deathly still. The servants paused in their work and looked up at their lord in surprise.

"It is gratifying to see so many friends who've come here tonight to celebrate the return of my son from the brink of death. As you can see, he's as he was before his fall." Merrick deposited the lad on a wooden bench beside Allegra. "It pleases me, too, that you come to give thanks to the one who healed him."

He took his place on the other side of his son, then motioned for the servants to continue passing platters of food and filling goblets. At once the guests bent close, for now there was more to speculate about. The room was abuzz with the fact that the lord had publicly thanked the witch.

"Do you think she's bewitched him?"

"And why not? It's what you'd expect from the likes of her."

"She's dangerous, I tell you." An old woman

studied the way Allegra was smiling down at Hamish, and laid her hand on the arm of her husband seated beside her. "Mind, now. Don't look her in the eye, Rupert. She'll steal your will."

The old man winked at his neighbor, seated across the table. "I might be more than willing to do her bidding, as long as she'd turn that sweet smile on me."

"I was thinking much the same," his neighbor said with a laugh. "The witch is easy on the eye."

While the two men shared a grin, their wives watched Allegra as one might watch a predator poised to attack.

One of them whispered, "For all we know, she could be an old hag who's taken on the guise of a beautiful young maiden in order to charm unwitting victims."

"If that be a hag," her husband replied in a voice that carried the length of the table, "I'd willingly be turned into an ancient, toothless old grandfather."

That had every man laughing, and every woman glowering.

"So, Hamish." Mordred sipped his ale and looked across the table at his nephew. "You're feeling rested?"

"Aye." The lad beamed a smile at his father. "I gave Mistress MacDonald my word that I'd eat more than I did this morrow when I broke my fast. She said I hadn't eaten enough to keep a bird alive.''

"It takes a while for the appetite to sharpen after being ill." Merrick returned his son's smile. "Give it time, lad."

"But it's already returned, Father." Hamish turned to Allegra. "The potion you gave me has made me hungry."

"That's good." She closed a hand over his.

"Potion?" Merrick's eyes narrowed. His hand holding the goblet paused halfway to his mouth, causing some of the ale to slosh over the rim. He took no notice.

Allegra shrugged. "Merely some crushed herbs."

"Such as?" Merrick's voice frosted over.

Though Allegra was aware of the sudden mood shift and the keen interest of the others at the table, she kept her voice level. "Feverfew. Mint. Chamomile. All are restorative and soothing, and should allow Hamish to sleep this night without dreams."

While she spoke, Allegra accepted a joint of fowl from a servant and cut off several pieces, placing them in the lad's trencher, along with an assortment of greens.

Mordred watched as his nephew ate every morsel. "I'd be careful if I were you, lad. After such a long time without food, you're apt to make yourself sick with all that."

"Should I worry, healer?" Hamish watched hungrily as Allegra filled his trencher again.

"Nay, Hamish. We'll not overdo it. But you need food to restore your strength."

Several times she cut pieces of fowl, and each time he ate all she gave him.

Finally he turned to her with a knowing smile. "Now may I have my reward?"

"You may indeed." She broke a biscuit in half and drizzled honey over the pieces, before offering them to him.

While he eagerly popped the first into his mouth, Merrick glanced over his head to say accusingly, "You bribed him with honey?"

Allegra merely smiled. "Where's the harm, my lord?"

Merrick's brows drew together in thought. "How is it you knew Hamish loved honey drizzled over his biscuits?"

Allegra looked down at her food, avoiding his eyes, for she was no good at deception. "Don't all little boys love sweets, my lord?"

Merrick nodded grudgingly and began to eat, though it was now his turn to have little appetite. He had no choice but to trust the woman. But it gave him no peace of mind. For the truth was, despite her knowledge of herbs and potions, and the fact that she'd already brought Hamish back from the brink of death, he was put off by the ease with which she slipped from a normal demeanor into witchery. She'd read the lad's mind. He'd lay gold on it. She probably knew things about him that even Merrick didn't know.

It galled him, but he had no defense against it, since he needed her so desperately.

Needed her.

It stuck like a stone in his throat to need anyone, but especially this witch.

As the silence stretched between them, Allegra felt a chill. There it was again. It was here. Close by. Possibly at this very table. The darkness. The evil. She glanced over to see Merrick glowering at her while Mara served his food.

Hearing the buzz of gossip around them, Mordred smiled at the young woman across the table. "What do you think of Berkshire Castle? Have you ever seen anything so grand?"

She pulled herself out of her dark thoughts, determined to remain cheerful if it killed her. "It seems grand, though I've had little chance to see more than Hamish's chambers and my own."

"I'm sure in the days to come you'll see all of it, and the village, as well." He glanced at his cousin, lowering his voice. "There are rumors that England's new queen will end up in the Tower like her mother."

Allegra shook her head. "Though I can sense Elizabeth living a long time, such things matter not to those of us who live in the Mystical Kingdom. Our isolation protects us from the world beyond our borders."

Merrick's tone deepened. "You'll rue such innocence if the English should ever decide to invade your peaceful kingdom, my lady."

"And why would they do that? We have nothing anyone would want."

He glanced at Mordred, who was staring at her with a look of disbelief. "If you think that, you're more innocent than you appear. Barbarians need have no reason to invade, other than the sheer pleasure they get from killing those weaker than themselves."

Allegra paled. "I have heard of men who kill for the pleasure of it. They carry a darkness in their souls."

Merrick looked out across the sea of faces in the great hall. "I wonder, my lady, what you would say to all the men in this room who have taken another's life on the field of battle. For myself, there are too many to count. Should I be judged harshly for that?"

She chose her words carefully, aware that his young son was listening. Her tone gentled. "You are a warrior, my lord. Yours is a noble calling, for you willingly risk your own life to protect the innocent.''

Mordred chuckled. ''What if my cousin takes pleasure in the killing?''

She saw Merrick's eyes darken with sudden anger. But the question, now asked, hung between them.

Very deliberately she forced herself to look into the darkness in the lord's eyes. What she saw brought a sense of relief. ''No matter what others think, you do what you must out of a sense of honor.''

Mordred arched a brow. ''You speak as though you know my cousin.''

''Nay. We are little more than strangers. But some things are impossible to hide.''

''What things?'' Mordred demanded.

She looked up. And felt a shudder pass through her. Why did she feel such unpleasant sensations with Merrick's own kin?

''I ask again.'' Mordred's tone was pure ice. ''What things are impossible to hide?''

Allegra took a moment to compose herself before saying, ''A pure heart and an evil one.''

''And you claim to see into a man's heart?''

''I make no claims.''

After that, though the others at table made several attempts, their conversation was strained.

Allegra was relieved when, a short time later, Mordred said, "Come, Desmond. It's time we mingled with our cousin's guests."

Allegra watched the two brothers walk away, Mordred in the lead, Desmond, towering over him, following like a docile child. Soon they were swallowed up by the crowd, which, after many goblets of their host's fine ale, had grown increasingly vocal.

A little later Allegra looked up to see Mordred approach the lord's table, trailed by a cluster of men and their ladies.

He made a slight bow before Allegra. "There are several in our midst with ailments, my lady. They beg a favor of you."

Merrick frowned. "The lady is my guest, Mordred. I expected better of you. I'll not have you making sport of her."

Mordred's expression never changed, though his eyes darkened with unspoken anger. "My request is sincere, cousin. And the lady is, after all, a healer." He turned to Allegra. "Would you not be remiss if you left these good people to suffer needlessly?"

She could see the challenge in his eyes, and wished she could flee his trap. Because of the goodness in her heart, she tried to see the same in others. Perhaps this man didn't know what he was asking. Though he thought to entertain himself and others,

Mordred couldn't know the price she would have to pay for his little game. Nor, apparently, did he care.

Scanning the faces, she turned to an elderly gentleman who was standing off to one side, as though embarrassed to be part of this crowd. Before she could stop herself, her heart went out to him. "You, sir, are suffering from a very painful throat."

After recovering from his surprise he nodded. "I am. And it's most vexing."

"Make a tea of thyme. It will soothe and heal your throat. On the morrow you'll feel much better."

He gave her a smile. "I thank you, my lady."

She returned the smile. "You're most welcome, sir."

"Can you cure my headache?" A plump, balding man stepped forward, leaning on a walking stick.

His wife stepped up beside him, glaring. "How can this woman do what no one else can?" She turned to Allegra. "He's suffered from them for a lifetime. They seem to be getting worse these past few years."

Allegra touched her fingertips to his forehead and frowned. "Aye. You're suffering now."

The old man nodded, while beside him his wife caught his arm, hoping to draw him away.

Allegra closed her eyes and let herself go into his

pain. Minutes later she stepped back, visibly drained.

He turned to his wife. "Why, the pain is gone. In the blink of an eye it disappeared."

The older woman touched his arm. "Did it? Truly?"

"Aye." He turned back to Allegra and caught her hand in his, lifting it to his lips. "Bless you, my lady. For the first time in years my pain is gone."

Though his wife was reluctant to touch a witch, she managed a slight bow of her head. "I thank you."

A murmur rippled through the crowd in the great hall, sending them pushing and shoving to get close to the lord's table.

"What about me?" One of the village gossips bullied her way to the front of the crowd, elbowing several aged and infirm members out of the way.

"We have not met." Allegra studied the matron poured into a gown of pink silk, waist nipped, bosom heaving, looking for all the world like an oversize pink sausage. "I am called Allegra Drummond."

"I am Lissa MacDermott." The woman, who was breathing hard and dabbing at her brow with a lace handkerchief, smiled at the others, clearly relishing the chance to be the center of attention.

"Where is your pain?" Allegra asked.

"Here." The woman touched a hand to her chest, enjoying the way the men gaped. "With each step I take, I can hardly breathe."

Allegra caught the woman's hands in hers and stared deeply into her eyes. "Do you truly wish to be cured?"

Lissa gave a smile of triumph to her friends before turning her attention to Allegra. "I do."

"Then you must do exactly as I say. When you go home tonight, you must remove the corset that binds you, and let out the seams of your gowns. I assure you, you will never again have trouble breathing."

At her words the crowd began roaring with laughter.

"Oh! You evil, horrid witch." Hearing the laughter, the horrified woman pushed her way past her neighbors and fled the great hall, with her husband running to catch up with her.

Merrick wiped a tear of laughter from his eyes as he whispered to Allegra, "I was wrong to worry about you. I should have known you would not tolerate fools."

Allegra merely gazed out over the crowd, wondering if any others would dare to test her.

Seeing Hamish stifle a yawn, Merrick put an arm around the boy. "You grow weary, my son?"

"Aye, Father."

"Then I'll fetch Mistress MacDonald. She can take you off to your bed."

Allegra seized the opportunity to escape. "Your housekeeper is too busy for that, my lord. She has your guests to look after. If you have no objection, I'd be happy to take Hamish to his room and stay with him until he's asleep."

His tone sharpened. "There will be no more potions?"

"None tonight. Though I'll not promise beyond that."

He gave her a long, thoughtful look before nodding. "Very well. You may see to the lad."

He kissed his son and watched as Hamish put his small hand in Allegra's. As the woman and boy made their way from the great hall, heads craned and, as before, a ripple of excitement raced through the crowd.

Mordred watched until the woman and boy exited the room. Then he turned to his cousin. "You'd best beware. The lad seems to be growing fond of the healer."

"And what's wrong with that, cousin?"

"You know nothing about her. You'd be wise not to trust those potions she gives him."

"I'll keep a close eye, Mordred."

Desmond leaned closer, his voice trembling with

unease. "What have you learned about her, Merrick?"

"Other than the fact that she knows how to entertain a crowd?" Mordred gave a short laugh.

Merrick's eyes darkened with anger. "That was unwise of you, cousin. I did not bring the healer here to be played a fool."

"I meant no harm." Mordred and his brother exchanged a look. "Desmond fears and mistrusts the witch. To put his mind at ease, tell us what you've learned about her, cousin."

"Little enough." Merrick stared down into his ale, his tone rough with impatience. "Though she is either the most innocent maiden in all of Scotland, or the most clever of all witches."

They fell silent as the village minstrel stepped into the center of the room and began to play his lute.

The crowd listened attentively while he sang of great battles, brave warriors and love-struck maidens. Though Merrick usually enjoyed such entertainment, this night he found himself distracted by thoughts of the healer. She'd seen his son's weariness as the perfect excuse to remove herself from this pack of curious onlookers. But the truth was, the minute she left the great hall, the magic of the night had gone flat.

In just this short time he'd begun looking forward

to being near her. Hearing her voice, and the musical trill of her laughter.

It wasn't only his son who'd grown fond of the healer.

That knowledge brought him no pleasure. In fact, it shamed him to admit that he was falling willingly under the spell of a woman he knew to be a witch.

Chapter Nine

"Will you tell me a story, Allegra?" Hamish lay, warm and cozy, in a nest of fur.

"Aye. What would you like to hear?"

"Tell me about your home."

She drew the shawl around her shoulders and settled herself beside his pallet, taking his hands in hers. "I live in a place called the Mystical Kingdom. It's a grand place, with soft, gentle weather and colors so vivid, they dazzle the eye. The grass is lush and green, and the flowers grow as tall as a man."

"Who lives there with you?"

"My mother, my grandmother and my two sisters, Kylia and Gwenellen, as well as a sweet old woman named Bessie and a troll named Jeremy."

"A troll? What does he look like?"

Allegra smiled at the boy's sudden interest. "He's no bigger than you, with fierce black eyes and long dark hair that must be trimmed often so he won't trip over it.''

That had Hamish giggling. ''What else?''

''He wears a frock coat and top hat that my mother made him. And though he may be frightening to some, he has a child's pure heart and a kind and generous spirit.''

Hamish took a moment to digest that before asking, ''Have you no father?''

She shook her head. ''He died when we were just babes.''

''How did he die?''

''He died defending my mother.''

''Someone wanted her dead?''

''Aye.''

''Why? Was she evil?''

''Nay. But they thought she was evil. There is a difference, Hamish. There are those who are truly evil, and there are those who are believed evil because they travel a different path in life. My mother, like her mother before her, has gifts that make some people afraid of her.''

''What sort of gifts?''

''She has knowledge of healing plants and herbs. She has the power to calm the wind, and ruffle the waters of the loch. And when I or one of my sisters is in peril, she feels it.''

''Do you have those powers, too, Allegra?''

"I have some of those powers. As do my sisters."

"And do people fear you?"

"Some do."

"Would they try to kill you?"

"They might."

His voice grew sad. "My mother is dead."

"Aye. So I've heard."

"She wasn't evil, Allegra. Why did she have to die?"

"We all must die, Hamish."

"Do you think she had any gifts?"

"I'm sure of it."

"I never saw her calm the wind or ruffle the waters." His little face became animated at the thought. "What sort of gifts do you think she had?"

"My mother told me that the greatest gift of all is love."

At once he nodded. "My mother loved me."

"You see? That's a fine gift she gave you. And one you can pass on."

"I can? How?"

"By loving as openly, as generously as your mother loved you."

He thought about it a moment before saying softly, "I love my father."

"You see? You're already passing on your mother's gift to others."

The thought of it had him smiling. "Will I love others the way I love my father and mother?"

She patted his hand. "Perhaps you will some day."

"Do you love anyone, Allegra?"

She nodded. "My grandmother, my mother and my sisters."

"Have you no husband or children?"

"Nay."

He imitated her, patting her hand gently. "Perhaps you will some day."

"Oh, Hamish." She bent and kissed him. "You are the dearest lad. Now…" She smoothed the blankets and sat back. "Close your eyes and I'll stay right here beside you until you're asleep."

"Will you sing to me?"

"If you'd like." She began to croon a lullaby that her mother had often sung. Her soft, musical voice washed over him, soothing away the last of his fears.

In scant minutes his breathing had gone soft and easy as he fell into a deep sleep.

Allegra got to her feet. Smoothing down her skirts, she turned and gave a gasp of surprise at the darkened shadow in the doorway.

"My lord." She clapped a hand to her mouth. How long, she wondered, had he been standing there watching and listening? Why hadn't she sensed his presence there?

As she started around him he stopped her with a hand on her arm. His voice was deep with feeling. "It was never my wish to publicly humiliate you, or to parade you in front of the villagers for sport."

She tossed her head. "If you say so."

"I do. On my word as lord. I wanted you there tonight for the lad's sake." And for mine. The thought taunted him.

"Very well. I believe you." Again she started past him.

Again he stopped her with a touch. Only a touch, but he could feel the heat burn a path of fire that went straight to his loins.

He stepped back, his eyes fierce. "What am I to do about you, Allegra?"

"Do, my lord?" She stood very still, wondering at the odd sensations swirling inside her at the touch from him.

"If you were a mere woman, I could trust my feelings. But you're a…" He saw her lips tighten, and swallowed back the hateful word. "Forgive me, my lady." He made a slight bow and stepped out of her way. "I'm keeping you from your sleep."

She lifted her head in that infuriating manner and swept past him like a queen. He'd thought he could let her walk away. And he would have, if his temper hadn't taken over his common sense.

Just as she reached the doorway of her chambers

he caught her by the shoulders and turned her to face him.

His face was contorted with barely controlled rage. "Have you cast a spell over me?"

"A spell?" Her eyes went wide. "What are you saying?"

"I believe you've bewitched me. It's the only explanation for what's happened to my mind."

She shook off his hand. "What's in your mind is your business, my lord."

"Is it? Is that what you think? I'm not so certain of it anymore." He took a menacing step closer and she backed up into the room until she could feel the wall at her back. "Since Catherine there's been no woman whose name I could even recall for more than a night. And yet I left my guests below stairs because I couldn't stop thinking about you. Why, Allegra?"

The look in his eyes was frightening to behold. Because she had backed up as far as she could, she lifted her chin in a show of bravado. "Why do you ask me? Surely you don't believe that I can control your behavior."

"If only I could believe that." His hand snaked out, snagging her wrist. That was his first mistake. Now that he was touching her, he couldn't seem to stop. He brought his other hand to her shoulders, but instead of keeping her at arm's length, he drew her fractionally closer, his eyes burning into hers. "I must taste your lips again, Allegra."

"Nay." She tried to draw back, but she was no match for his strength. In one fluid movement he dragged her against him, nearly lifting her off her feet as he covered her mouth with his.

There was temper in the kiss. Hers as well as his. As heated, as potent as a blow from an enemy's sword. He reveled in it, allowing it to fuel the mix of passions that had been seething for so long now. He felt the heat pour into him, adding to the flames. At the roar of blood in his temples he lifted his head, unable to believe what he'd just experienced. His head was still spinning. His body vibrated with need. How could one little female cause such feelings?

Allegra went very still, struggling to calm her ragged breath. How could she possibly fight this man's magic? With just one touch he could melt her bones. With but a kiss he could turn her blood to fire. He had the power to steal her will so that it was impossible to resist him.

But resist him she must.

She tossed her head. "You've no right to take such liberties. You'll leave my chambers at once."

Instead of a reply he dragged her into his arms once more, determined to silence her protest. But this time, when his mouth covered hers, the hands at her shoulders gentled, as did his kiss.

Once again he tasted the sweetness, and was drawn to it until he was drinking his fill. He lingered over her lips, drawing out the kiss until she sighed and, without realizing it, wrapped her arms around his waist and clung.

Was the room turning in lazy circles, or was it her brain? Had the floor dipped and tilted beneath her feet, or was it her body vibrating? She neither knew nor cared. All that mattered was this man, this kiss, this absolutely amazing moment.

If he'd continued to treat her with arrogance, with temper, she could have fought it. But this tender side of him left her helpless. It was all she could do to keep from moaning with the pure pleasure of his kisses.

He felt the change in her and thrilled to it. Despite her innocence, he could taste the awakening of desire. He could feel the heat growing around her, inside her, drawing him in.

He changed the angle of the kiss and took it deeper. Then he caught her arms and lifted them to encircle his neck. When he brought his hands down her arms, along her sides, his thumbs encountered the swell of her breasts.

At her quick little intake of breath he soothed her with soft gentle touches along her back, all the while feasting on her lips, until once more she relaxed and allowed him to touch her at will.

She was such a delight. Hesitant, yet bold. An innocent seductress. A witch who seemed completely unaware of the power she held over him.

Right now that power was leading him down a dangerous path. The rush of desire caught him by surprise. The need to take her had the blood curling hotly through his veins. A wise man would end this now, before they both crossed a line. But how could he be wise with this woman in his arms? How could he think, when the taste of her had him drunk with desire?

He lingered over the kiss a moment longer, then, gathering his strength, lifted his head, breaking contact.

He heard her quiet sigh of frustration and was warmed by it. Perhaps he hadn't been the only one lost in the moment.

He took a step back. "I'll leave you now as you ordered, my lady, and return to my guests below stairs."

He turned and walked to the staircase. His hand on the banister, he noted, was still vibrating from the touch of her.

Allegra closed the door to her chambers and leaned against it, waiting for the weakness to pass. Then she made her way on trembling legs to the chaise drawn before the fireplace, where she sank down gratefully.

Each time Merrick touched her, kissed her, his magic grew stronger and hers grew weaker. She had no defense against it. And what shamed her even more, she didn't care.

She closed her eyes and laid her head back, lost in thought. If Merrick hadn't found the strength to walk away, she would have allowed him to stay, to take whatever liberties pleased him. For there were forces here beyond her control. He was the one with the power. And she was helpless against it.

In the darkened hallway a shadowy figure paused outside Allegra's chambers. It was as feared. Merrick MacAndrew was drawn to the witch.

Another complication.

The wife had been a simple enough matter. She'd been weak and fanciful. The son was no better. A lad that wee would soon have been disposed of. But this woman had power and magic on her side. Potent strengths.

Still, if the healer were to be found dead in the lord's own castle, perhaps in his bed, would there be anyone left to believe his protestations of innocence?

Perhaps it was just as well that Merrick had lived through the dangers of the Mystical Kingdom, and had returned with the healer. Now he would be humbled before his people, and stripped of all his power before facing the ultimate challenge.

In her chambers Allegra felt a shadow pass over her, leaving her chilled. Getting up quickly, she hurried to the door and peered into the darkness of the hallway, but could see nothing. Still the feeling persisted. The darkness, the evil, were here in this place.

She undressed quickly, then climbed into her pallet, pulling the furs around her to ward off the lingering chill.

Just as she was beginning to doze, she felt someone in the room. Fearful, she sat up and peered into the darkness. As she got to her feet and scurried across the room, she heard footsteps. Lifting a flaming stick from the coals, she whirled to face her intruder.

The room was empty.

She raced to the doorway and peered into the darkened hallway, but could see nothing.

Long into the night Allegra lay, unable to sleep. Part of it was the fear of the evil she could sense here at Berkshire Castle. But another part of her restlessness, she knew, was that scene with Merrick MacAndrew.

What was she to do about the lord? Worse, what

was she to do about these strange new feelings that had her so unsettled?

His magic was diminishing hers. And that could be deadly, especially since she had the feeling that someone here at Berkshire Castle wished her great harm.

She could leave at any time. She was no longer a prisoner here. And yet, in a strange way, she was still a captive of Merrick MacAndrew. He had somehow taken over her will, causing her to foolishly embrace his cause, and that of his sweet, innocent son.

If she were wise, she would put a shield around her heart before it was too late. But considering how her heart behaved whenever the lord of Berkshire Castle was near, it was probably already too late for that.

Chapter Ten

"Good morrow, my lady." The housekeeper looked up to see Allegra descending the stairs with little Hamish in tow. "Where are ye off to with that basket on ye'r arm?"

"I thought Hamish and I would walk in the garden, and if he's feeling up to more, perhaps we'll investigate the meadow beyond for herbs."

"Mara could see to the herbs if you'd just tell her what ye'd like."

"Mara?"

"The wench has some knowledge of field herbs for cooking. She could fetch what ye need."

Allegra shook her head. "I thank you, Mistress. But I find the fresh air invigorating. I think it will be good for Hamish, as well."

Remembering his last walk in the garden, the old woman couldn't hide her concern. "I don't think it wise. Nor would the lord, if he knew."

"I'll keep the lad close to me, Mistress MacDonald. Hamish will never be out of my sight."

The housekeeper eyed her suspiciously before ruffling the boy's hair. "Have ye'r walk, then. When ye return, I'll have Cook prepare ye'r favorite biscuits and broth."

The boy gave her a smile and clung to Allegra's hand as they walked out of the keep.

Allegra could feel the hostile stares from the servants as they passed. No one, it seemed, was willing to trust her with the lord's son. Or perhaps their concern was really for themselves. They viewed her as the enemy, and they had formed a wall to keep her out.

Once in the garden they walked slowly along a stone pathway, pausing occasionally to smell a perfect rose, or to watch birds splashing in the fountain that stood in the middle. Scattered here and there were stone benches set among the trees and flowers.

Allegra drew in a breath. "Oh, Hamish, with a little effort this could be such a lovely place."

"It was my mother's favorite spot in the keep. Sometimes I think I recall sitting here with her in the afternoon, waiting for my father to return from the village."

"It's good to have those pleasant memories, isn't it?"

"Aye." He gave a wistful sigh. "I wish I could remember more."

Allegra chose a stone bench set beneath an ancient tree with gnarled branches that formed a canopy of shade. "Let's sit here awhile and enjoy the view." As they sat she noted the lad's pallor. "Do you grow weary?"

"Aye, my lady. I need a moment to catch my breath."

She nodded. "The time spent in your bed has left you a bit weak. But the more you walk, and begin to play again, the stronger you'll grow."

"I pray it's so." He drew up his feet and rested his chin on his knees. "I wonder which tree I fell from?"

"You've no recollection?"

He shook his head. "None. Will it come back to me?"

"It will." She drew an arm around his shoulders. "You must give it time, Hamish. Soon enough the memories will come flooding back."

They looked up to see Merrick strolling toward them, trailed by his cousins.

Merrick frowned and forced himself not to stare at the way Allegra looked, her hair windswept, her cheeks pink from the sunlight. He'd spent the longest night of his life, thinking about the way she'd felt in his arms. Hours later he could still taste the sweetness of her lips. It had been torture to think about her, all the while wondering if she'd given him any thought at all.

"When Mistress MacDonald told me you were in the garden, I grew concerned, lad." He glanced beyond the boy to Allegra. "I'm not sure my son should be out here so soon."

"Aye." Mordred nodded in agreement. "You know what happened the last time he attempted to walk in the garden."

Hamish looked up, shielding the sun from his eyes. "What happened?"

Before anyone could stop him Mordred knelt in front of Hamish. "You took a spell in the garden, lad. It happened when you were walking with Mistress MacDonald."

"A spell?" The lad's brows knit together. "There seem to be so many things I can't remember."

"No matter." Annoyed, Merrick nudged his cousin aside and ruffled the boy's hair the way the housekeeper often did. "Your healer brought you out of it."

Mordred got to his feet and gave Allegra his most charming smile. "You're an amazing woman. Those parlor tricks you played last night for my cousin's guests were most entertaining."

Hamish swiveled his head to stare at her in surprise. "Were they tricks, healer?"

"They were not tricks, Hamish." Allegra's tone frosted over as she regarded Mordred. "But it seems you were amused."

"Oh, indeed I was." He caught Hamish's hand. "Since you're here for the air, why don't we walk a bit, lad?"

The boy glanced over at Allegra. "The healer promised to stay by my side. Will you come with us?"

She managed a smile, despite her anger at the man beside him. "Of course I will. As long as you promise to tell me when you've grown too weary."

Allegra got to her feet and followed behind Merrick and Mordred, who kept Hamish between them. Though Desmond walked beside her like a towering hulk, he spoke not a word as they followed along a stone path that led deeper into the garden.

Spying some feverfew, Allegra paused to pick some, placing them in her basket.

"Planning a potion?" Mordred watched as she straightened and smoothed her skirts before joining them along the path.

"Perhaps."

Merrick indicated the basket. "What is the weed good for?"

"It's a calmative. It uplifts the spirit of those who drink it in tea, or even wear it braided about the wrist."

He chuckled as he glanced at her wrists. "I see you have no need of it."

"I've no need of calming. But I thought it might give Mistress MacDonald some relief from her nerves."

"I see. Do you intend to heal everyone in Berkshire Castle, my lady?"

"I won't refuse any who ask."

"Truly?" Mordred stopped to glance at her. "And if I should ask for a potion so that a certain lady will warm to me, could you provide such a thing?"

She paused to add lavender and marjoram to her basket. "I know nothing about affairs of the heart."

"You mean there weren't a score of lads knocking on your door in the Mystical Kingdom?"

Allegra paused to inhale the fragrance of a rosebud, then knelt to pluck some pennyroyal to add to her collection. "None."

The little boy turned to look up at her adoringly. "No one but Allegra's family lived there."

Mordred arched a brow. "A pity you were kept in such isolation, my lady. That explains why you seem so removed from the things of this world." He gave her a measured look before turning to his cousin with a knowing smile. "But I'm sure you'll find a man willing to teach you how to use your hidden feminine wiles."

Allegra plucked several stems of rosemary. "I much prefer honesty."

Mordred laughed. "Honesty is not part of a lover's game."

Allegra paused. "Do you consider love a game?"

"Exactly. Love requires losing one's heart. As for mine, it's never been touched, so how can it be lost?"

"I've had enough of such foolish talk." Merrick's harsh tone had the laughter dying on his cousin's lips.

Seeing Merrick's frown, Mordred took a step back. "Aye. I'd forgotten about your sense of honor, cousin. Desmond and I are off to the village. We've errands to see to." He patted little Hamish on the head and surprised Allegra by catching her hand and lifting it to his lips. "I thank you for the pleasure of your company, my lady. It has been most entertaining. I do hope we can do this again soon." With a sly smile he added, "Perhaps I could show you the rest of the gardens before we sup tonight."

Before she could refuse he strode away.

Merrick stared after him. When he turned back, his eyes were as dark as thunderclouds. "I had no idea you and my cousin had become such good friends." He lifted his son in his arms. "It's time you returned to the keep, Hamish. Cook has biscuits and broth ready."

"What about Allegra?" The boy reached out a hand to her, but Merrick moved away. "The lady's basket is only half-filled. I'm sure she has things she'd rather do than watch you eat."

"I don't mind..." Allegra's words faded as Merrick stormed away, carrying his son in his arms.

Within minutes they had disappeared inside Berkshire Castle, leaving Allegra alone in the garden.

As she wandered around filling her basket, she thought about Merrick's puzzling behavior. Last night he'd been so tender, she'd begun to believe that she'd misjudged the man. Today he was behaving once again like the half-crazed lout who had stormed her kingdom and had spirited her away.

Men, she thought as she left the garden and began walking across the meadow. Her life in the Mystical Kingdom had been so much simpler without them.

"Ale, m'lord?" The housekeeper paused beside Merrick, who stood in front of the fireplace in the great hall staring glumly into the flames.

"Aye. Thank you." He accepted the goblet and glanced around. "Where are my son and the healer?"

"They'll be along in a little while. The lady wanted the lad to drink some tea before he sups."

"Tea?" Merrick's frown returned. "Another potion?"

"Aye, m'lord. But the lad didn't seem to mind. He said it was tasty enough."

"Tea made of weeds." He turned to the old woman. "Have we all lost our minds?"

"Like you, I was quick to judge, m'lord. But I've heard from the servants that the only topic of conversation in the village is the lady who can heal their ills. Tavish's sore throat is gone, after drinking a tea made of crushed thyme. Logan's headaches have fled since the lass laid her hands upon him. There are dozens more clamoring to have the lady cure their ills."

He gave a hiss of annoyance. "All of this distracts her from the reason she is here. I care not about anyone except young Hamish."

The old woman shook her head. "Ye don't mean that, m'lord."

At his sharp look she colored. "Oh, I know ye risked life and limb to bring her here to cure ye'r son. But I don't believe ye're as uncaring about all the others as ye claim to be."

He shrugged and emptied his goblet.

As the old woman lifted a decanter to refill it, he asked, "What's this you're wearing tied about your wrist, Mistress MacDonald?"

Her flush deepened. "Feverfew, m'lord. The healer said it would soothe and calm me."

"And does it?"

She replaced the goblet and started across the room. "I've only just begun wearing it, m'lord. We'll see what it brings on the morrow." She looked up and brightened. "Ah. Here are the lad and lass now." In an aside she muttered, "Ye've kept the lord waiting, my lady. Ye know he prefers to sup at sundown."

"Aye. Thank you, Mistress MacDonald."

"Will I pour you some ale before I go?"

"There's no need, Mistress. I'll see to it myself." Allegra followed Hamish across the room. "Good evening, my lord."

He nodded a curt greeting. She looked as pretty as one of the roses in the garden, in a gown of pale pink, with her flame hair spilling down her back in a riot of curls twined with ribbons.

"Allegra says the fresh air has put color in my cheeks, Father." Hamish tugged on his father's sleeve to get his attention. "What do you think?"

Merrick tore his gaze from the woman to glance down at his son. "I believe she's right. You look as healthy as a warrior."

"I do?" The boy beamed at the unexpected compliment.

"Aye. I think your little jaunt may have been good for you."

Allegra poured ale into a goblet and turned.

"Then perhaps you'll join us on the morrow when we take the pony cart to the village."

His frown was back. "Do you think that's wise?"

"Hamish was complaining that he hasn't seen his friends in a very long time. I thought that perhaps if they saw him, and realized that he was recovered from his fall, they might be persuaded to visit the castle and play with him."

"I'll not have him climbing trees."

The boy's eyes widened. "You mean never again?"

"Aye. That's what I mean, lad. Look what happened to you last time. Do you think I'd let you take such a risk again?"

"You can't mean that, my lord."

At Allegra's words, he slammed down his goblet, sending ale spilling over the rim. "I say what I mean, and mean what I say, woman. I love my son too much to ever see him hurt again. I forbid him to run with the village lads and climb trees, or go off to the forest, where harm can befall him."

"So you'd keep him here, hidden away in the castle for the rest of his life, rather than risk his being hurt?"

"If I must. And who's to stop me? I'm lord of Berkshire. My word is law. And I'll not have some—" He was about to call her a witch again, until he caught himself in time. "Some tart-tongued female telling me what's right or wrong for my son.''

Hamish looked from his father to the healer, wondering at the sudden flare of anger.

When the housekeeper came scurrying into the room to announce that dinner was to be served, she caught sight of the fire in the lord's eyes and beat a hasty retreat.

Minutes later, when the servants entered bearing trays of food, Merrick stiffly held a chair at the table for Allegra to his right, and Hamish on his left, before taking his seat at the head of the table.

Allegra picked at her food, uncomfortably aware of the way Merrick watched her.

"Fresh bread, my lady?"

Allegra accepted a slice from the servant.

"More mutton, my lord?"

Merrick refused more, leaving the servant gaping. Never had the lord been known to refuse a second piece of meat.

"More ale, m'lord?" Mistress MacDonald hovered about nervously.

"Aye." When the housekeeper filled his goblet halfway, he shot her a dark look until she obligingly filled it to the top.

Hamish looked over. "I've finished my meal, Father. May I have a biscuit now, drizzled with honey?"

"Aye, you may. In your chambers."

"But I—"

"In your chambers, boy. Now."

As the boy shoved away from the table, Allegra did the same.

Merrick snagged her wrist. "You will stay."

She glanced at the lad. "But Hamish—"

"Will go to his chambers with Mistress MacDonald." He shot the housekeeper a dark look.

Without a word the old woman caught the boy's hand and led him from the room, ordering the servants out as she did.

When they were alone, Merrick leaned back, sipping ale and regarding Allegra. "How was your walk in the garden with my cousin?"

"I refused his kind offer. I wanted time to prepare a tea for Hamish. The lad is, after all, the reason I'm here."

At her words he tried not to let his pleasure show. He sat back and regarded her. "You find fault with my desire to keep my son safe."

"Nay. Not with your desire to keep him safe. Only with your method. You would lock him away, thinking you can keep the world out. But all you will do is keep him from becoming the man he most admires."

"And who would that be?"

"You, my lord."

He stared down into his goblet to hide his pleasure. "You think that by flattering me you can soften the blow? I'm not a man to be admired. I am a warrior who has killed men in the field of battle. A husband who couldn't keep his wife safe. A father who fled his only son rather than face the difficult task of raising him alone."

Allegra studied him, amazed at his admission. "You judge yourself too harshly, my lord. I've seen how others regard you."

He looked up. "And how is that?"

"They speak of your courage on the field of battle. More than once you've put yourself between a wounded man and an opponent's sword. As for your son, I've seen you with him. You're patient and kind and loving."

"And in your opinion, overly protective."

She sighed. "Perhaps a bit."

"Tell me something." He set the goblet on the table and regarded her. "You say that locking away the ones we love for their own protection is wrong?"

She nodded. "I do."

"Then how do you explain the fact that, in the name of love, you and your sisters were spirited away to an isolated land far away from those who might wish you harm?"

For the space of a minute Allegra was too stunned

to speak. Finally finding her voice, she shoved away from the table. "It isn't the same."

"Isn't it?" As she started away he caught her roughly by the arm and turned her to face him. "I thought at first you were merely feigning innocence. But your kisses tell me otherwise. You're a woman, Allegra Drummond. With a woman's feelings. And yet you have no defense against them, because you've been so sheltered."

"You see things that are not there. I have no feelings for you, Merrick MacAndrew. Therefore I need no defense."

His voice went dangerously soft. "Would you like me to prove you wrong, my lady?"

She pulled free and backed away, her eyes wide with fear. "I forbid you to touch me, to kiss me, the way you did last night."

"You forbid? You forbid?" With a snarl of temper he dragged her roughly into his arms and lowered his head, covering her mouth with his in a punishing kiss.

At once the heat poured between them, with all the flash and fury of a storm, heating their blood, searing their flesh. Neither of them would have been surprised to see lightning dance across the ceiling, or hear thunder echoing across the halls. It felt as if the entire fortress shuddered from an assault.

Allegra wanted to fight him. But the minute his

lips were touching hers, the weakness came over her again, leaving her trembling with need.

How could one man's mouth be so clever? The mere touch of his lips to hers had her hot and cold and filled with such confusing feelings, her poor head was spinning.

He continued kissing her until she could feel the blood throbbing in her temples. She feared at any moment she would ignite and burn to ash.

A whimper escaped her lips and he lifted his head. For a moment he struggled, as though pulling himself back from a deep, dark cavern.

His eyes were hot and fierce and frightening in their intensity. "Leave me."

"But I…"

"Leave me, woman. Now."

Her legs were trembling so badly, she feared she might fall as she stumbled toward the door.

"And Allegra."

At the deep timbre of his voice she turned.

"Before you retire this night, put a brace to the door of your chambers."

"Aye." Though she didn't understand the reason for his sudden violence, she fled without a word.

Allegra awakened from a sound sleep with the prickly sensation that someone was outside her door. She sat up, eyes wide with fear, as the handle turned.

The brace held, and though the door moved enough to cause sparks in the fireplace to dance, it remained firmly closed.

She slipped out of bed and listened at the door to the sound of footsteps receding.

Shivering, she crossed the room and tossed a fresh log on the embers, watching as flames began to lick across the bark. Hugging her arms to herself, she pondered who might wish to enter her chambers while she slept, and why. It could have been a servant, wishing to stoke the fire. Or it could have been someone else, with a more sinister purpose.

She had many enemies in this place. In truth, she feared that she had not a single friend.

She climbed beneath the furs and lay listening to the sounds of the night. The sooner she helped young Hamish recover his memories, the sooner she could return to the safety of the Mystical Kingdom. To that end she would pour all her energies. For if she didn't soon leave this place, she feared not only for her heart, but also for her very life.

Chapter Eleven

"**M**'lord." The housekeeper bustled into Merrick's chambers, wringing her hands. "I must speak with ye."

He refused to look up from the ledgers that had occupied all of his energy in the past few days. He'd locked himself away, cool and distant with everyone in the keep. "What is it, Mistress MacDonald?"

"It's the healer. She's in the garden, digging in the dirt."

"Aye? And what's the problem?"

The old woman seemed startled. "It isn't right, m'lord. She's doing the work of a servant."

"If that's her choice, so be it."

"There's more, m'lord."

Merrick gave a hiss of impatience. "Out with it, Mistress."

"She has the lad working with her. His little

hands and knees are filthy. The two of them are wallowing in the mud like...like...barbarians.''

He pushed away from the massive desk and swept past the old woman with a sigh of disgust. ''I'll see to them.''

Merrick made his way to the garden, but saw no one around. Just as he was turning away he heard a trill of laughter. Using the sound as a guide, he followed one of the garden paths until he came to a strip of land just beyond the garden, in a meadow filled with wildflowers. The earth had been neatly turned, and tender young plants had been set out in orderly rows. At the end of a row he saw Allegra and Hamish, kneeling side by side.

''Did I do it right, Allegra?'' The little boy sat back in the dirt while the woman beside him turned to examine his work.

''Oh, aye. Are you certain you've never worked a garden before?''

Hamish caught sight of his father and got to his feet, flushed with pleasure. ''Look. Allegra is allowing me to help her plant her herbs.''

''I see.''

Allegra stood, brushing down her skirts, avoiding his eyes. ''I thought after I'm gone an herb garden would be useful for the household.''

Gone. The word did something strange to his

heart. He'd refused to allow himself to think about the inevitable.

"Allegra's teaching me the names of all the plants, and what they're good for." Hamish idly rubbed the dirt from his hands. "We've already planted savory, thyme, sage and rosemary, and as soon as we can find some young plants, she said we'll add chamomile and mint."

Merrick turned to her, fighting to keep any emotion from his tone. "And how do you propose to keep the forest creatures from eating your tender plants?"

"When we've finished planting, I'll make a wattle fence woven of sticks and green willow branches. That should keep the creatures at bay."

He couldn't help but admire her resourcefulness. "It would appear that you've thought of everything."

Merrick was fascinated by a smudge of dirt on her cheek. He wondered how she would react if he were to lean close and wipe it with his finger. Still, in truth, he didn't trust himself to touch her, and so he curled his fingers into fists at his sides. "Why didn't you ask the help of some of the servants?"

She shook her head. "That wouldn't be fair to Mistress MacDonald. She needs their help in the keep. Besides, I enjoy working the soil, and I thought it would be good for Hamish to learn how to care for his own needs.''

"You sound like my first instructor. When Mordred, Desmond and I were being trained, we were taught that a warrior must be able to see to not only his own needs, but also those of the men he leads. And so we were each taken to a different spot in the forest and told to hunt our food, prepare it, find a safe place to sleep and to return within a fortnight as either leaders or followers.''

"What did you do, Father?"

Merrick smiled at his son. ''I dug a pit and started a fire, then went off and killed a stag with my dirk. While it roasted, I went in search of Desmond, fearing he was too slow-witted to survive. I found him huddled in the branches of a tree and brought him back to my camp. The next day Mordred wandered in, cold and hungry.''

Allegra glanced over. "How old were you?"

"Nine years.''

Allegra had no time to react before Hamish caught his father's hand and led him along the neat rows. "Look, Father.'' He began reciting the names of all the plants, and the many illnesses they could cure.

Allegra trailed behind, deep in thought. What oddly divergent lives they had lived. While she had been safe and complacent in her Mystical Kingdom, this man had been learning the tasks of a warrior while still a lad. There had been no time for childhood pleasures, such as fishing in a stream or swimming in a loch. Instead he'd learned how to place his own life in jeopardy for those he loved.

When they came to the end of the row Merrick knelt, so that he and his son were eye-to-eye. "You don't find the work tedious?"

"Is this work?" Hamish seemed genuinely surprised. "Allegra told me it's play."

"And you believed her, lad?"

"Aye. 'Twas as much fun as climbing trees."

Merrick's eyes narrowed as he absorbed a twinge of guilt. "Do you miss the climbing?"

"Aye."

"And you truly wish to climb again?"

"Aye, Father. When I'm stronger, and you give your consent."

Merrick lowered his head, considering. "Then I promise to think on it." Without taking time to change his mind he added, "Now, what do you say we take the healer into the village?"

The boy clapped his hands. "In the pony cart?"

"If you'd like."

"Oh, aye." Hamish looked down at himself, then at Allegra's filthy gown. "But we'll have to wash."

"That you will. I don't believe you'd like the entire village to see the two of you looking like beggars.''

''Come, healer.'' Hamish caught her hand. ''Let's hurry and wash so I can show you the village of Berkshire.''

As she danced away beside the boy, she could feel Merrick watching, and was surprised by the little thrill that raced along her spine. At once she dismissed the feeling. It wasn't caused by the man. After all, since that night he'd ordered her away, he'd kept to his room, refusing to join them even for meals.

Nay, it wasn't the man. It was merely the knowledge that she would get to see something of his world before returning to hers.

''Well, you certainly look better than when I saw you last.'' Merrick brightened when his son came dancing down the steps of the keep toward the waiting cart. Perhaps he'd been wrong to worry about the lad. He seemed fit and healthy, and there was good color to his cheeks.

''Up you go,'' he called as he lifted Hamish to the wooden seat.

He turned to Allegra, who was busy wrapping a shawl around her shoulders. Before she could look up, he had her in his arms, lifting her up.

Seeing the flush that stole over her cheeks, he

couldn't resist leaning close to whisper, "Light as a feather you are, my lady. And though I'm loath to admit it, you feel good in my arms."

This light, almost playful mood was so out of character, Allegra could make no response. She was settling herself on the seat when Merrick pulled himself up beside her.

Hamish seemed delighted. "You're going to drive the cart yourself, Father, instead of riding your horse alongside?"

"Aye. What need have we of a servant?" Merrick accepted the reins from a young stable lad and gave them a flick. The horse started off, with the little cart moving smartly along the curving path that led to the village.

Hamish turned to Allegra. "Father says when I'm bigger, he'll let me handle the reins."

"Won't that be grand?" She dropped an arm around the lad. "But it won't be enough. As soon as you're old enough for that, you'll want to be even bigger, so that you can do more grown-up things."

"Aye. Like wielding a sword, and going off to do battle with the invaders."

At his words, she saw Merrick look over at the lad. His tone was gruff. "Don't be in such a hurry to grow up, lad."

"Weren't you, Father?"

He nodded. "Aye. But times were different. After

losing my father in battle, I wanted more than ever to be able to protect my mother. I'd have willingly given my life to keep her safe.''

Allegra felt a rush of tender emotions for the man beside her. ''When I was nine years my life was so serene. My greatest worry was whether my garden of herbs would survive a drought.''

Merrick flicked her a glance. ''And did they?''

She felt the rush of heat from his gaze, and became aware of his thigh pressed to hers on the hard seat. Though she held herself stiffly, their shoulders brushed as he worked the reins. With each touch she could feel the heat that passed between them.

''Aye. My garden thrived, and my days remained simple and carefree.''

''Then perhaps your mother was wise to spirit you and your sisters off to your Mystical Kingdom. For our lives here in the Highlands have been rife with war.''

''You make me feel guilty for my life of peace, my lord.''

He closed a hand over hers. ''It is never my intention to burden you with guilt, Allegra.''

Perhaps it was his touch, or the tone of his voice. Perhaps it was the fact that he called her by name. Whatever the reason, she felt her heart flutter like a caged bird.

''It's the sort of life I want for Hamish, as well.

It's what every parent wants for his child. What every man wants for the people he cares for.''

There was such passion in his tone. She could understand why his people had chosen him as their lord. She had no doubt that he would willingly lay down his life for every person under his protection.

As they moved along the trail they spotted Mordred and Desmond in the distance, their swords glinting in the sunlight.

Allegra shielded the sun from her eyes. ''Are they fighting?''

Merrick chuckled. ''Merely honing their skills as warriors.''

''But why? Don't they get enough of that when they engage in battle?''

''Most warriors do. But it's different when you've lost a father to the invaders. Then you feel that you must always be ready to face the enemy.''

''Do you feel that way?''

He shrugged. ''Perhaps not as much as my cousins. You see, they lost not only a father and mother, but their home, as well.''

''But you've opened your home to them.''

''How could I not? Their father was brother to my father. They know they will always have a place with me and mine.''

Allegra continued watching the glint of their

swords until they were out of sight. Again she felt a chill, as though a shadow had passed over the sun.

She was grateful when they rounded a bend and found themselves in the little village of Berkshire. Up ahead she could see crowds of people milling about the square.

"So many people."

"Aye. It's market day. As a lad, this was always my favorite day."

"As it was mine." Allegra smiled. "It's one of my earliest childhood memories of the time before we fled to the Mystical Kingdom."

Merrick brought the horse and cart to a halt and helped Allegra and Hamish to the ground. As Allegra was smoothing down her skirts an old man hobbled over to grasp her hand.

With a crowd of curious onlookers watching from a safe distance, he said, "My lady, I drank the tea made of thyme as you suggested, and my throat, which had been sore for more than a week, was instantly healed."

Her smile bloomed. "I'm glad I could be of some help to you, sir."

"'Twas more than help." His voice had others looking over. "I told my wife it's a miracle." He bowed grandly over her hand, which he lifted to his lips. "I thank you, my lady."

His words had the crowd surging closer, staring in silence.

Allegra drew an arm around Hamish's shoulders as she followed Merrick toward the booths, filled with squawking chickens and geese, bleating lambs, bits of lace and embroidery, and tables laden with biscuits and sweetmeats.

She approached a table where an old woman sat hunched in her shawl, the needles in her hands clacking in rhythm as she knitted a fine tunic.

The old woman's head came up sharply. "Are you the one they call the healer?"

Allegra paused in midstride, aware that the crowd had gone very quiet. "I am."

"I've heard of your deeds." The fingers had ceased their work.

Allegra stepped closer, peering into the cloudy eyes. Her voice softened with tenderness. "How long have you been without sight?"

"All my life."

Allegra caught the gnarled hands in hers. "It is my fondest wish that I could work miracles, but I haven't the power. All I can do is heal that which is wounded."

The old woman reached out, tracing her fingertips over Allegra's face, pausing at the arched brow, then moving across the high cheekbones, down the curve of jaw, outlining the pursed lips.

"I've no need of a cure, my lady. I've lived all my life in darkness. Surely the light would cause me great pain after all these years."

By now the crowd had surged forward, eager to hear everything, for the old woman was known to be a wise old seer.

Her voice rose and carried in the silence. "But even without the gift of sight, I sense a heart that's pure and clean and untouched by the evils of this world."

At her words the people began murmuring among themselves. They watched in amazement as the old woman wrapped her arms around Allegra's shoulders and drew her close, whispering something for her ears alone.

When Allegra turned away, there were tears in her eyes.

Alarmed, Merrick touched a hand to her arm. "What is it, my lady? What did the old crone say to cause you pain?"

Allegra merely shook her head. "It's nothing. Just the kindness of a stranger." She took in a deep breath to compose herself before saying, "I believe this tunic is the perfect size for Hamish. What say you, my lord?"

He placed a bag of coins in the old woman's hands. As he reached for the tunic she whispered, "My lord, the lass is a special gift that you must treasure. But beware. See that you guard her with great care.''

After thanking her, he moved on, watching the way the crowd now embraced both Allegra and young Hamish. As they moved from booth to booth, partaking of sweets, admiring bits of lace and stooping to watch the geese in their pens, the people milled about, exchanging pleasantries and even daring to touch her as she passed.

The crowd swelled to even greater numbers, and Merrick caught sight of his own cook and several of the castle servants visiting the booths. At one such booth, while several people gathered around Allegra, the servant Mara was smiling as she handed Hamish a sweet. The lad devoured it in a single bite.

Though Merrick forced himself to enter into the spirit of the day, strolling with his son and Allegra, calling out to friends and neighbors and even lifting a tankard with the men of the village, he couldn't get the words of the old woman out of his mind.

Was she entreating him to enjoy the treasure and partake of the healer's sweetness for his own pleasure? Or were the words meant as a warning that danger was near?

He shrugged off his uneasiness. The old woman had always spoken in riddles. He had neither the time nor the patience to unravel this latest one.

* * *

The blazing sun had crossed the sky and now lay on the horizon, casting the land in shadow. At a touch of the reins, the little pony cart veered from the path and danced across a meadow.

Allegra turned to Merrick. "Why have you chosen a different route?"

He shrugged. "I thought I'd show you as much of the countryside as I could. Just beyond this meadow another path intersects, leading us back home."

He glanced at the fields of heather. "I've always loved this place. It's where I played as a lad, and where later I was given my first lessons in a warrior's skill with broadsword, dirk and longbow."

Allegra noted the sword in its scabbard and the glint of the knife's hilt tucked at his waist. "Do you really need those weapons just to visit the village on market day?"

He turned to her with a look of surprise. "Do you think the invaders give a warning before attacking? Look around you, woman. Those trees could be harboring an army of barbarians. Even the fields of heather can hide the enemy, lying amid the blossoms, waiting for the moment. Danger can strike with no warning. It can lurk in a peaceful meadow, just as it can in a Highland forest. The wise man is always on guard against the unknown, unseen enemy."

"Forgive me, my lord. I meant no…" Allegra's words faded as Hamish fell against her with the weight of a boulder. Instinctively her arms came around him. "Quickly, my lord. Stop the cart."

Even as she shouted the words, she was fighting to keep the lad from falling. It took all of her strength to hold him, for he had once again left all that was warm and comforting and had slipped away into that other world.

Chapter Twelve

Merrick brought the cart to a sudden, lurching halt and leaped down before circling to the other side and taking the boy from her hands. As he laid him in the heather he was forced to watch helplessly as Hamish's body began twitching violently.

He looked up, his voice a hoarse cry. "Help him."

"Aye." Allegra dropped to her knees beside the lad and placed her fingertips on his temples. As she connected with him, she could feel one emotion overriding all others. Fear. It coursed through his veins like icy fingers, leaving her chilled and shaken.

"What is it?" Merrick looked from the boy's face to hers. "What do you feel?"

She shook her head. "He's afraid."

"Of what?" Merrick touched a hand to the hilt of his sword. "If you but show me the thing that frightens him, I'll gladly slay it."

She sighed. "If only it were that simple, my lord. I doubt even Hamish can put a name to his fear. Something he saw, or heard, caused a glimmer of memory. But only a glimmer. As yet, it has taken no form in his mind. At least, none I can discern."

"Can you help him? Can you bring him back again?"

She closed her eyes. "I can try." She moved her fingers in slow circles, sharing with the lad her strength and her calm center.

As the tremors ceased and his body stilled she began chanting the ancient words.

Merrick sat back on his heels, watching and listening. The words, which were now becoming more familiar to him, soothed, though he knew not why. Everything about this healer was soothing. Not just the gift she used so generously, on behalf of others, regardless of the cost to her. It was more her easy acceptance of those things beyond her control. The very fact that she was here, fighting for his son, gave him comfort. If anyone could heal the lad in mind and body, it was this woman. He felt it with absolute certainty.

It seemed an eternity before the fluttering eye movement behind closed lids heralded a return from that other world. At last the lad's eyes opened and he stared up at Allegra and Merrick with a look of confusion.

"What has happened? Was it the…spell that Mordred spoke of?"

"Not a spell. It was more a sleep." Allegra sensed that the boy needed to move beyond the fear of the unknown. A spell was a fearsome thing, but to a lad, sleep was normal and natural. "Did you eat or drink anything today that might have weakened you?"

"I drank some goat's milk, and shared a sweet or two with the servants."

"Can you think of something that might have caused you to be afraid, Hamish?"

He shook his head and sat up weakly. "I know not." Then his gaze was captured by the cluster of tall trees behind them. He stared in fascination. "Could those be the trees I was climbing when I fell?"

Allegra arched a brow and glanced over her shoulder. "They could be. Perhaps we could ask Mara, to show us where it happened."

"And if this isn't the place of the accident?" Merrick asked. "What then?"

Allegra shrugged. "It could have been something Hamish heard. A word. A phrase that unlocked a memory."

"Think, Hamish." Merrick touched a hand to the lad's shoulder. "Can you recall anything at all?"

The boy seemed afraid to search too deeply. Instead he looked up at his father. "May we please go home now?"

"Aye, if you feel strong enough to sit." Merrick took the boy in his arms and placed him gently on the seat, then settled Allegra beside Hamish.

As he caught up the reins, he noted with satisfaction that the healer had lifted the boy onto her lap and was holding him close to her heart.

There had been another who had loved the lad, and cuddled him close. And now she lay in a grave.

A shudder passed through him, and he was reminded of the blind woman's words. He'd been foolish to dismiss them so lightly. As the fortress came into view he whispered a solemn vow to do all in his power to keep the healer and the lad safe from anything that might threaten to harm them.

In the courtyard Merrick handed over the reins to a stable lad and took Hamish from Allegra's arms.

As he entered the keep, Mistress MacDonald hurried forward. The minute she spied the lord carrying his son she gave a little cry of distress. "Now what's happened to our lad?" She began wringing her hands. "Don't tell me he's fallen?"

"Nay, Mistress. He's merely weary."

The old woman gave a sigh of relief. "Cook made special honeyed biscuits to welcome ye back home, m'lord."

"Be certain to thank her." Merrick started up the

stairs, then paused as a thought struck. "Instead of the great hall, we'll take our evening meal in my chambers." He glanced down at his son. "How does that suit you, lad?"

"Will we be alone? Just you and the healer with me?"

"If you like."

"Aye." The boy wrapped his chubby arms around his father's neck, feeling suddenly safe and warm and content. "I'd like that, Father."

"It's done, then." He turned to the housekeeper. "See that there's a fire laid on the hearth at once."

By the time he and Allegra walked into his chambers, half a dozen servants were scurrying about. A table was being set in front of a roaring fire. A chaise, covered with furs, was placed to one side.

Merrick set his young son on the chaise and covered him with fur before handing him a goblet of hot mulled wine.

"Here, lad. This will warm you."

He offered a second goblet to Allegra, who accepted it gratefully.

As she walked close to the fire, Merrick studied her, noting her pallor. He kept his voice low enough that the lad couldn't overhear. "Forgive me, Allegra. In my fear for my son, I'd forgotten what this does to you. Perhaps you'd prefer to retire to your chambers."

She shook her head. "I'm just a bit chilled. The fire and the wine will soon enough work their magic."

"You're the one with the magic, my lady." He regarded her over the rim of his goblet. "I can't bear to think what would have become of Hamish without you."

"You mustn't dwell on it, my lord." Without thinking, she laid a hand on his arm and was stunned by the warmth that rushed through her veins.

As she started to pull away, Merrick closed a hand over hers. His eyes burned into hers with a brightness that held her even when she tried to look away. "You feel it, too, don't you, Allegra?"

"I know not what you're saying."

"Don't you?" His eyes narrowed. He leaned close. "You can't deny the heat that sparks between us whenever we touch."

"I know not…"

"Here ye are, m'lord." Mistress MacDonald came rushing headlong into the room, trailed by the servants bearing a feast fit for royalty.

Merrick's head came up sharply and he was forced to step aside, watching with impatience as the meal was arranged on a sideboard.

When all was in readiness, the servants stood back while Merrick, Allegra and young Hamish took their places at the table. Then the servants, under the direction of the housekeeper, began filling plates and goblets, before being sent away, leaving only the housekeeper to serve them.

Determined to put the old woman at ease, Allegra said, "I must remember to ask Cook what she does to get the mutton so tender."

"She'd be pleased to tell ye, m'lady. 'Tis a source of pride to her."

"As well it should be. My mother and grandmother will be happy to learn that I've developed an interest in cooking, since they'd despaired of it ever happening."

The old housekeeper gave her a shrewd look. "Most lasses take no interest in cooking until a lad comes along to snag their heart. Then they think of ways to please him. Could it be there's a lad on ye'r mind, m'lady?"

As Merrick turned to study her, Allegra could feel herself blushing clear to her toes. For a moment he simply enjoyed the high color on her cheeks as he said, for her ears alone, "I hope to heaven it's someone I know."

That only caused her blush to deepen.

To spare her any further embarrassment, he bit into a biscuit and turned to Mistress MacDonald, drawing attention away from Allegra. "I believe Cook has outdone herself. You'll convey my thanks, Mistress."

The old woman nodded. "Aye, m'lord."

If she wondered at the lord's uncommonly thoughtful behavior, she gave no indication. It occurred to her that everyone at Berkshire Castle had undergone some changes since the arrival of the healer.

As yet, she hadn't decided if the changes were for the better or the worse.

"Cook baked honeyed biscuits for the lad. And for ye, m'lord, sugar cake dotted with currants." She served him a huge slice, drizzled with heavy cream, which he devoured within minutes.

Then she stood back, enjoying the way the lord and his lad took similar pleasure in their sweets.

As for Allegra, she nibbled a small slice of currant cake and smiled her approval. "Cook has indeed outdone any expectations I might have had. I hope you'll convey my thanks, as well."

"I will, m'lady."

When they'd eaten their fill, Merrick returned his son to the chaise before signaling for ale. At once the old woman filled a tankard and offered it to the lord before calling for the return of the servants.

When the table was cleared and the servants took their leave, the housekeeper lingered. "Would ye care for anything else, m'lord?"

"Nay, Mistress. I thank you for your service."

She blinked, as though uncertain whether or not

to believe what she'd just heard. Had the lord actually humbled himself to thank her?

She gave a slight bow. "It's my pleasure to serve ye, m'lord." She turned to Allegra. "I'll say goodnight now, m'lady."

"Good night, Mistress MacDonald."

When they were alone Allegra glanced over to see Hamish stifling a yawn. "Would you like me to take you to your chambers?"

He shook his head. "Just a few minutes more, please."

She turned to Merrick, who nodded.

The little boy patted the chaise. "Will you sit here, Allegra, and tell me more about your home?"

"If you'd like." She settled herself beside him, tucking her feet under the furs. "What would you like to know?"

"Do you have your own horse?"

"Aye." She smiled at the memory. "Sunlight. He is a lovely golden winged horse with silvery mane and tail."

"Winged?" The boy looked astonished. "You mean he can fly?"

"Indeed. I still recall the first time I climbed upon his back. He soared so high I feared we were headed for the sun. But he merely swooped all around our lovely kingdom, then settled down right where we'd started. It was a most delightful experience, and one I've enjoyed many times since.''

''Can he fly you to faraway places, as well?''

She shook her head. ''He can't leave the Mystical Kingdom. If he were to leave, there would be hunters hoping to ensnare him for profit.''

''If I were to visit your kingdom, would Sunlight take me flying?''

''I don't see why not. As long as your father has no objection.''

''Would you, Father?''

Merrick had listened to this in utter silence. It confirmed what he'd suspected. And yet it sounded so improbable, he wondered how such a thing would be regarded by others. Except for children, with their wild imaginations, and those few like him who'd actually visited the Mystical Kingdom, it seemed like something out of a dream. But it was no dream. He'd seen these winged horses, even though at the time he'd questioned his own sanity.

He sipped his ale. ''I should think it would be great fun to ride a horse across the sky.''

''You'd let me ride Sunlight?''

''I suppose, as long as Allegra assured me he would bring you no harm.''

''He's a very gentle creature.''

Gentle. Merrick studied the young woman reclining beside his son. Nothing in this world could be more gentle, nor more sweet. And right this moment he wished he could take her into his arms and fill himself with her sweetness.

He felt the jolt to his heart and stared down into his ale to veil his thoughts.

"Do your sisters also ride Sunlight?" Hamish had dozens of questions whirling through his mind.

Allegra shook her head. "They have their own winged horses."

"And your mother and grandmother?"

The young woman gave a mysterious smile. "They have no need of such things, for they can fly of their own accord."

Merrick's head came up sharply. His eyes narrowed.

Hamish seemed delighted. "You've seen them fly?"

Allegra nodded. "Aye."

"They have wings?"

"Nay." She was quick to explain. "They have no need of wings, for they don't exactly fly. They simply…appear."

"How?" The boy was clearly enchanted.

"I know not. For it's one of the gifts my sisters and I fail to possess."

"No matter." The lad patted her hand. "It's enough that you have a winged horse that lifts you into the sky." He closed his eyes, trying to imagine such a wonder. "I hope I can visit your kingdom and ride Sunlight."

"I would enjoy showing him to you." She brushed the hair from his forehead and pressed her cheek to his. "You would love my home and family, Hamish."

When the little boy didn't reply, she lifted her head and looked down at him. His eyes were closed, his breathing slow and easy.

She slid from the chaise and called to Merrick, "The lad's asleep."

"I'll carry him to his chambers." Merrick set aside his tankard and lifted the boy in his arms.

With Allegra trailing behind, he carried Hamish down the hall and into his room. As soon as he laid him down, Allegra covered him with a fur throw and brushed a kiss over his cheek, as though she'd been doing so for a lifetime.

Merrick felt a rush of tenderness at the sight.

When they exited the lad's room, they walked together along the hallway until they came to Allegra's doorway.

Before she could step inside, Merrick touched a hand to her arm. Feeling the rush of heat, he quickly lowered his hand to his side. "Thank you, my lady."

She paused. "For what?"

"For all that you do to comfort my son." He

shook his head and turned away. "You'll never know how frightened I was, seeing his little body twisting and writhing in pain."

Without thinking, she pressed her hand to his back. "You mustn't dwell on it, my lord."

At her touch he flinched, and she withdrew her hand quickly. In that same moment he turned and caught it between both of his. The heat that had flared moments earlier now became a flame that neither of them could ignore.

She tried to step back, but his hands at her shoulders stopped her. She looked up into his eyes and wondered at the hot, fierce look in them. As though with but a glance he could devour her.

They both looked up as Mordred and Desmond appeared at the top of the stairs.

"Here you are, cousin." Mordred was smiling broadly. "We've been awaiting you in the great hall."

"And drinking great quantities of ale, it would seem." Merrick, furious at this latest distraction, narrowed his eyes on the men. Was his entire household conspiring against him?

"Aye. That we have." Mordred glanced from Merrick to Allegra. "It would seem we've interrupted the lord, Desmond." He touched a hand to Merrick's arm. "Will you join us below stairs?"

Merrick's mouth was a thin, taut line of repressed

fury. "Aye." He continued looking at Allegra. "Go now. I'll be there shortly."

He could feel the two men watching him before they turned on their heels and descended the stairs, laughing together.

When they were gone Merrick stepped back. "Now I'll warn you, my lady, as I did the other night. Close your door and put a brace to it."

"I don't understand."

He turned away, determined to put as much distance between them as possible. "There are times when you don't need to understand. It is enough to do as I bid, for I am lord of this fortress." His tone was rough with anger. "Now bar your door, lest the ale weaken my brain and have me storming your chambers later."

Without another word he was gone, striding down the stairs like one possessed of demons.

Though he hardly relished the thought of drinking with his cousins, it seemed wiser than what had originally crossed his mind.

Chapter Thirteen

Allegra entered her room and set the brace, then crossed her arms over her chest and paced in front of the hearth, deeply troubled.

Why was it that Merrick seemed always angry whenever they touched? His reaction was the exact opposite of hers. When he touched her, she felt herself melting. Her blood warming. Her heart swelling with strange new feelings she couldn't put into words.

And when he kissed her—the mere thought had her head swimming. When he kissed her, she wanted the kiss to go on and on, without end. Though it shamed her to admit it, she wanted him to touch her everywhere. There was something about his touch. At first it had frightened her. But now just thinking about Merrick touching her, kissing her, had the tingling starting anew.

With but a touch he could make her weak. With a single kiss she was unable to think, to reason.

She pressed her hands to her cheeks, feeling so alone. If only her mother were here. Or her grandmother. Those wise women would be able to help her sort through these troubling thoughts.

She paused at the balcony and stared at the stars winking in the night sky. Slowly the feeling came over her that she wasn't alone. Though her family was far away, they would hear and understand.

"Oh, Mum." She lifted her head and saw one star brighter than all the others. "What am I to do about these feelings? Would it be wrong of me to give in to them? The thought of lying with Merrick MacAndrew, of mating with him, is almost overpowering. But if I should mate with this man, would I forfeit my powers?"

As if in answer the star began to glow and glimmer in the sky. Rubbing her eyes, Allegra sank to her knees on the balcony and waited to hear her mother's voice. Instead, all she heard was the silence of the night. It washed over her, soothing, calming, until, exhausted, she slept.

Her sleep was filled with vivid dreams. Her mother, young and carefree, running across a meadow of heather toward a handsome man who stood with arms open wide. He caught her and lifted her high, then spun her around and around until she was dizzy and shrieking with laughter. She wrapped her arms around his neck as they kissed. Still locked in her embrace, he lowered her to the grass. At first she was uneasy. But with soft words and tender kisses he eased her fears until she joyfully embraced the love they shared.

Allegra awoke feeling oddly comforted by the dream. Her mother had loved a man. Loved him with all her heart. Despite their love, her powers had not diminished, but instead had grown stronger with the birth of each of her daughters.

Allegra looked around, wondering how long she'd been lying here in the cold of the balcony. When she made her way inside, the fire was still ablaze on the grate. Had it been mere minutes?

She went very still, wondering if she had actually dreamed it, or if her mother, sensing her daughter's uneasiness, had sent the images to ease her mind.

"Oh, Mum." She clutched her arms about herself and stared into the fire. "Thank you for giving me a glimpse of you and Father. I'm overjoyed to know I'm not alone in these feelings. They're not unique to me, but are experienced by all who love." She lowered her head to study the toe of her slipper, wondering just what she should do with this newly discovered knowledge.

She hated this ignorance. She, who knew so much about growing herbs and forest plants, about working the soil and healing bodies and minds, hadn't a scrap of knowledge about men and women and how they dealt with their emotions. Should she go to Merrick and confess her feelings? Or were such things better kept locked away in her heart?

She closed her eyes and struggled to reach out to her mother and grandmother, knowing they would have the answers to all of these questions.

Merrick sat slumped in a chair by the fire, a tankard of ale in his hand. At his feet the hounds dozed.

Mordred stood to one side, his hand resting on the mantel. "So, Merrick. How much longer do you intend to keep the witch here?"

"What is that to you?" Merrick drained his tankard and Mordred was quick to fill it.

"The men have begun to talk."

"About what?"

"About the fact that you've changed since the witch came here. There was a time when you were the strongest warrior in all the Highlands. Now you seem content to fill your days with walks in your garden and visits to the market."

Merrick was out of his chair, his hand twisted into the front of his cousin's tunic. "You would dare say such things to me?"

Mordred wrenched free and took a step back.

"Someone has to tell you what is being said behind your back."

Merrick turned to Desmond. "And you? Do you say such things, as well?"

Desmond shrugged.

Mordred set aside his tankard. "We've both heard the whispers."

"Whispers?"

Mordred glanced at his brother with a sly smile before nodding. "Some say you've grown soft. They say you're…bewitched."

"Do you think that?"

"I think you are concerned for your son, as would any man be." He looked up and touched a hand to Merrick's arm. "But you are lord of all the people. You can't permit your fears for your son to allow our borders to be overrun with invaders."

Merrick's tone hardened. "I see no invaders taking over our land. How dare you suggest that I am cheating my people?"

Mordred lifted his head. "Think on this, then. You may have to resign yourself to the fact that the lad suffered damage in the fall that will continue to cause these…spells. And if that is true, then the best thing you can do is send the witch back now, before she fills his mind, and yours, with foolishness." He waited a beat before adding, "Unless, of course, there is some other reason why you refuse to send her back to her home.''

''What other reason?'' Merrick's eyes flashed a challenge.

''I think you know, cousin.'' Mordred picked up his tankard and drained it, wiping his mouth with his sleeve. ''She's easy to look at. Why not simply pleasure yourself with her and be done with it?''

''That's your way, not mine.'' Merrick's nostrils flared. ''Since we were lads you've boasted about bedding every wench in the village.''

''And have, I assure you.'' Instead of the expected denial, Mordred seemed inordinately pleased with himself. ''And then there are the lasses I've met in the neighboring villages. They can't resist my charms either, it would seem, for I've planted my seed from mountain to valley. And you could do the same, cousin, if you'd give up that damnable notion of a warrior's honor.''

''You think it honorable to bed women for sport, Mordred?''

''Can you think of a better one?'' The haughty young warrior shot his cousin a demonic grin. ''Why not pleasure yourself with the witch if you fancy her? Then send her packing and get on with the business of leading our people. Unless, of course, you'd prefer to grow old in your garden and let another be lord of the people.''

Instead of a reply, Merrick slammed down his tankard and turned on his heel, striding from the hall.

Mordred watched, then turned to Desmond with a thoughtful look. "It's worse than we thought. He doesn't simply want the healer. I believe he's lost his heart to her." He threw back his head and laughed. "Fool. The woman's a witch, and before she's through with him she'll have him so blinded by love he'll not see the enemy at his own gate. But then, that's to our advantage, brother. If our cousin is too addled to see, his enemy will at last have the upper hand."

Merrick slammed into his chambers, discarding his plaid on the chaise. As he stalked toward the fire, he tore off his tunic and hurled it into the corner of the room. With a series of muttered oaths he stubbed off his boots and kicked them against the far wall.

His hands were at the fasteners of his breeches when he caught a slight movement by the balcony. In swift strides he was across the room, shoving a figure against the stone while the dirk in his hand pressed against a throat.

"Allegra." The fury was still there, too hot to control. The knowledge that he'd been seconds from slitting her throat had him trembling. "By all that is holy, woman, what are you doing in my chambers?"

"My lord." The words came out in a strangled cry.

Even when he lowered his hands, she cringed away from him, hugging herself to the cold stone of the balcony. She'd never before witnessed such white-hot anger in a person, and had no defense against it.

"I ask you again." His eyes narrowed on her. "Why are you here?"

"I need to know what magic you possess, my lord."

He looked stunned. "Magic? That I possess?"

"Aye." She swallowed, struggling to calm her racing heartbeat. "Each time you touch me, I feel it. This incredible heat. And this weakness that comes over me. Even my mind is affected. When you get too close, I can't think."

He made a sound that might have been a laugh or a sneer. "And all along I thought it was your magic at work here."

She shook her head. "I have no magic that compares with yours. Tell me what it is."

He glanced at the knife in his hand before setting it aside on a chest. His hand was still shaking. He flexed his fingers before curling them into a fist. "It is merely the wanting of a man and a woman. Some call it lust.''

''Nay. I know of that word. This is something much deeper than wanting. Whatever the magic, it has taken hold of my heart and I know not how to break free. I find myself...'' She took in a quick breath for courage. ''I find myself wanting to lie with you, Merrick. To mate with you.''

Though her words shook him to his very core, he refused to acknowledge them. For to do so would be to admit to the same feelings of weakness. He turned away, dismissing her. ''You talk foolishness, Allegra. Go now. Leave me.''

''Foolishness?'' She stiffened as though he'd slapped her. ''Is that what you think? That because of my ignorance, I'm not to be taken seriously?''

When he kept his back to her, she took a step toward him, then stopped, lifting her head with as much pride as she could muster. ''Very well, my lord. You may reject what I offer. I have no way of comparing my feelings for you, since you are the first man to lay hands on me. Perhaps my blood would surge like this for any man. Perhaps any man's kiss would have the power to wipe my mind of all thought. Though I doubt it.'' Her voice lowered. ''But know this, Merrick MacAndrew. It isn't any man I want. It's you. Only you. And since you do not return my affection, there will be no other.''

As she started past him, he snagged her arm and turned her to face him. In the glow of the fire he could see the sheen of unshed tears that glistened in her eyes.

Not tears, he thought. Sweet heaven, the sight of them tore at his heart.

"Oh, Allegra." Without thinking, he caught her by the upper arms and drew her close, pressing his forehead to hers. "Your innocence, your honesty humble me."

She tried to pull away. "Don't make sport of me, my lord."

"Is that what you think?" He ran his hands up and down her arms, feeling the heat building between them. This time, instead of fighting it, he welcomed it, knowing it was the same for her. "I've tried to deny these feelings, because to give in to them would be to take advantage of your goodness and innocence, and that I would never do. I cannot forget that you're here because I forced you. It would be unthinkable to force you even more." He lowered his voice. "To take what you offer would be the greatest pleasure of my life. But the choice must be yours and yours alone."

"Are you saying that you…want me?"

His words came out on a moan. "Desperately. Though I've tried just as desperately not to show it."

"Oh, my lord." She leaned into him, offering her lips.

He took them with a hunger that startled them both, gathering her firmly against the length of him. His hands began moving over her while his mouth plundered hers until their breathing grew ragged. And still he lingered over her mouth, fighting the need to ravish her.

He lifted his head, pinning her with a long, probing look. "You have to be certain of this."

He saw the fear that clouded her eyes. But to her credit she straightened her spine. "I'm certain of but one thing, my lord. I'm willing to follow wherever you lead me."

He absorbed the quick rush of heat and thrilled to it. Still he held back, determined that the choice be hers, and hers alone. "And if you find yourself in more…passion and peril than you expected?"

She touched her hand to his cheek in an achingly sweet gesture that had him sucking in a breath. "I'll trust you to see me through it safely."

"God in heaven, Allegra." He closed his eyes and gave a low moan that might have been pleasure or pain. "What have I done to deserve such goodness as this?"

She stared up into his eyes with such trust, such adoration, he could feel his heart swelling. "Whatever we have done or not done, this thing between us is right and good, my lord.''

In answer his lips covered hers in a kiss so hot, so hungry, all she could do was cling to him as he took her on a wild, dizzying ride. When he lifted his head she reached up and framed his face, dragging it back for yet another kiss, unwilling to end the pleasure.

At last, their chests heaving, their breathing ragged, he whispered inside her mouth, ''You were warned, my lady. Now that the beast has been set free, there'll be no caging it.''

Chapter Fourteen

His mouth, that warm, clever mouth, covered hers in a searing kiss, while his hands, those rough, warrior's hands, moved over her, setting fires everywhere they touched.

She shuddered, helpless to do more than cling to him as he worked his magic. Once again he was clouding her mind, stealing her will. And this time she offered no resistance. This was what she wanted. What she desperately craved.

His tongue met hers, tasting, dueling, until she sighed from the pure pleasure of it. He lingered over her mouth, as though afraid he might never have enough of the taste of her.

Here was heaven. His own mystical kingdom, right here in these arms. Arms he never wanted to leave.

Just as she began to relax, his mouth dipped

lower, to press wet, nibbling kisses down her throat. With a lazy sigh she arched her neck and wrapped her arms around his waist to anchor herself.

For the space of a moment her hands stilled. He was naked to the waist, and the feel of his skin had her palms tingling, her heart racing. Then she allowed her hands to move over him, loving the feel of him.

Was the room moving, spinning? She felt it dip and sway and had to close her eyes to keep from being dizzy.

"I thought—" his mouth moved over her upturned face "—when first I felt these stirrings, that you'd bewitched me."

"And I believed the magic to be yours." She absorbed the warmth of him, the deep rumble of his voice inside her pores, and could do nothing more than sigh with the pure pleasure of it.

He framed her face and stared down into her eyes with a hot, hungry look that had her shivering with anticipation. "And now here you are, and I still think I'm bewitched."

"As am I, my lord."

"Oh, Allegra. My beautiful, bewitching Allegra. You've become so precious to me." He pressed moist kisses over her eyelids, her cheeks, the tip of her nose. "I'm such a brute, I'm afraid I'll hurt you."

She brought her hands to his arms, thrilling to the strength she could feel in them. "You could never hurt me, Merrick. You're too good."

"If you think that..." He sighed. "You're too trusting by far, my lady."

Then his mouth was on hers again, this time with a kiss that drained her even as it filled her. A kiss that engaged her fully, until she wrapped her arms around his neck and moaned with impatience.

He brought his hands down her arms, along her sides, until his thumbs brushed the fullness of her breasts. A pulse began throbbing deep inside, and she felt a rush of heat that left her weak and trembling.

"My lord." The words were torn from her lips.

"Hush, love." He lowered his head and his lips closed around her breast. Despite the barrier of her gown, she could feel the heat all the way to her core.

She was hot. So unbearably hot. And there was this powerful need building inside her. A need that had her body shuddering.

"I need to see you. All of you." He lifted his hands to the neckline of her gown and with one quick tug, tore it from her and tossed it aside. Then his fingers untied the ribbons of her chemise until it, too, fell away.

She saw the way his eyes gleamed as he looked at her. Whatever shyness, whatever modesty she might have felt was gone, replaced with pride at the knowledge that she was the one he wanted. The one he ached for. There was such love in those dark eyes as they remained steady on hers.

"My beautiful, delightful Allegra. You take my breath away."

Then his hands were on her, touching her, moving over her until she felt her legs grow weak and her knees begin to buckle.

At once he lowered her gently to his pallet, all the while kissing her until she could feel the breath backing up in her throat.

He leaned up on one elbow, studying the way she looked in the firelight. Flesh as pale and flawless as alabaster. Eyes gleaming like points of flame. That spill of fiery hair, inviting him to touch. And he did. Tangling his fingers in it while he ran hot, nibbling kisses over her face, her neck, her throat, then lower still, until she gasped and clung to him.

He brought his mouth to her earlobe, nibbling, tugging, until she chuckled at the unexpected sensations. But the laughter became a moan of pleasure when, with jagged thrusts of his tongue, he drove her slowly mad.

When his mouth returned to hers the heat between them grew, until their bodies were slick with sheen. And still he moved over her, kissing her breasts, then bringing his mouth lower, to the pale, white skin of her stomach, then lower still, until she moaned and writhed with need.

Sparks shot from the fire on the grate, though neither of them noticed. Outside the balcony a dove cooed to the moon, and its mate answered. The man and woman locked in an embrace neither saw nor heard. All they could see was each other. All they heard were soft sighs and whispered promises. And the uneven thundering of two hearts, lost in the wonder of newfound love.

The world had narrowed to this chamber, this pallet, this breathless moment.

Merrick could feel the change in her. No longer the shy maiden, she had become as caught up in the madness as he. Now at last he was free to do all the things that until now he'd only dreamed of.

With his mouth he took her over the first crest and gave her no time to recover before taking her up again on a wild, dizzying climb.

Allegra hadn't known what to expect. Tender kisses, perhaps. The feel of his rough hands on her smooth skin. But this was beyond her wildest dreams. Her body was on fire. Her mind was filled with so many exotic images, all of them wildly erotic. She'd never known a need like this. A hard, driving need that had her reaching blindly for him, needing to touch him as he was touching her.

As her hands moved over him, she heard his

moan of pleasure and was hungry for more. Drunk with need, she followed with her mouth until she felt him quivering. The knowledge that she was the one to bring him such pleasure was intoxicating.

This deeper, darker side of loving had her trembling. Her body was alive with needs. Desire as sharp, as vicious as the blade of a dirk had her hungry for more.

Her body arched toward him, her hands fisted in the furs beneath her. While she writhed and twisted beneath him, he slowly drove her closer and closer to the edge of madness. And still he held back, needing to draw out the pleasure. It was all he had to give her in return for the precious gift she'd offered him.

Against her mouth he whispered, "For so long I've dreamed of this. Of holding you. Of kissing you. Of lying with you. And now you're here, my love."

Love. The word wrapped itself around her heart, warming her as his kisses warmed her lips.

"Say the words, Allegra. Say that you're mine. Only mine."

She touched a hand to his cheek and stared into his eyes, fierce with desire. "I'm yours, my lord. Only yours."

The need for her was too great. The desire too

overpowering. He had to take her now, or explode from this terrible need ripping through him.

With his eyes steady on hers he entered her, then, at her sudden intake of breath, he went very still. "Sweet heaven, how could I forget that you're a maiden? Forgive me, my love."

"Nay." She smiled then, and wrapped herself around him, drawing him in deeper. "I want this, too, my lord. I want you. Only you."

"Oh, my sweet, beautiful Allegra."

Sweat beaded his forehead as he gave in to the needs that were clawing to be free.

Though he struggled to be gentle, it was too late for tenderness. Needs so long denied swamped them both.

Lungs straining, hearts thundering, they began to move, to climb. Pleasure, bordering pain, began to build until at last, locked in a fiery embrace, they stepped off the very edge. And flew.

They lay, still joined, cushioned by the pallet of furs. Neither of them could find a reason to move. And so they remained, waiting for their world to slowly settle.

Merrick lifted his face from the hollow of her throat and saw the glitter of tears on her lashes.

Tears?

With a rush of remorse he levered himself above her. "Forgive me, Allegra. I've hurt you."

"Nay." Though it was an effort, she lifted a hand to his face. Stroked. "I'm just overwhelmed, my lord."

He felt his heart begin to beat once more. "Truly? I didn't hurt you?"

She shook her head from side to side before asking, "Is mating always like this?"

He pressed his lips to her temple. "It can be. When the two who share such things care deeply for each other."

She traced the outline of his lips with her finger. "I care, my lord."

His lips curved. "And for that I'm most grateful, my lady."

"As am I." She lay there, loving the feel of his warm, slick body on hers. If possible, she would stay this way all through the night.

But surely he would want her to leave, now that he was through with her. The thought was so disturbing, she bit her lip as she contemplated how she should take her leave.

As she started to scramble up, Merrick caught her, stilling her movements.

"Where are you going?"

She looked away. "I'm sure you would like me to go to my chambers now."

"And why would I want that?"

"Because the...mating is over, my lord."

"Is that what you think, Allegra? That I would use you, and then send you away?"

She shrugged, keeping her gaze averted. "I know not, my lord."

"Oh, Allegra. My sweet, wonderful Allegra." He drew her into his arms and pressed his lips to her temple. "In this bed I'm not your lord."

"You're...not?" She pushed away to look at him.

"I'm simply the man who adores you." He smiled at the startled look in her eyes. "And mating is not a single act."

"It isn't?"

"Nay."

"What is it, then?"

"It's wanting to touch each other. Often. Intimately. And whisper silly endearments, just to see the other smile."

"You mean, saying you adore me?"

"Aye, my love."

Again that startled look that had his smile growing. "You see? You can't deny that you like it when I call you my love."

She blushed. "I do. But it isn't necessary to please me, my lor..." She swallowed. "It may take me some time to call you other than my lord."

He drew her close, staring deeply into her eyes. "Call me by my name."

She lifted her chin. "Merrick."

"Again."

"Merrick." Her tone softened. "Merrick, my love."

"Oh, Allegra." He gathered her into his arms and pressed his mouth to a tangle of hair at her temple. "My Allegra. My very own sweet, delightful, adorable witch."

As he drew her down, she gave a gasp of surprise. "Are we going to mate again?"

"Would you like that?"

She smiled. "I would. But I didn't know such a thing was possible."

He couldn't help chuckling against her mouth. "I am lord of the land. I declare that this night, in your arms, my wonderful witch, anything is possible."

And then there were no words necessary as he showed her, in the only way he could, that he was a man of his word.

Chapter Fifteen

"So many scars." Allegra lay nestled in Merrick's arms, running her hands over his chest, down his thigh. "Are they all from battles?"

"Aye." His voice was soft with contentment. After a night of loving, he was pleasantly sated. But as her hands moved over him, he could feel himself becoming aroused once more. How was this possible? It amazed him that this sweet innocent could be such a temptress. He would never have enough of her. She'd bewitched him, and he was too besotted to care.

She traced a thick line of knotted flesh that intersected another. "This must have hurt so."

"Aye. It was a lance that nearly impaled me. But I survived, as you can see."

"How can you bear to go back to battle, again and again, knowing you'll be forced to endure such pain?"

"I'd rather endure the pain than see my son in bondage to some barbarian."

She heard the thread of steel in his tone and understood his passion. "Does it not upset you that your own people call you the Sword of the Highlands?"

He shrugged. "I do what I must for the sake of my people. If they choose to think that I somehow enjoy the carnage, how can I stop them? I fight for their freedom, Allegra, as well as my own. And not just some freedom, but all. Even the freedom to think what they please about me."

"My fierce warrior. If they but knew the goodness in your heart." She touched a hand to his face and began tracing the curve of his brow with her finger.

He caught her hand and brought it to his lips. In the moonlight his eyes gleamed, hot and fierce. "How could I have known, when I stormed your kingdom and stole you away, what a treasure you would prove to be?"

She brushed her lips over his. "And if I'd known how my captor would steal my heart, I could have been spared some very frightening moments. I thought you would surely drown me in the Enchanted Loch."

He chuckled, remembering. "I nearly got us both drowned."

"You were a fearsome sight to behold. Covered with blood, and looking more like a giant than a mere man. How did you get past the dragon?"

"I slew him. But first I had to face that army of swordsmen who guard the loch."

Allegra looked puzzled. "My family employs no army."

"Perhaps it was arranged by your mother or grandmother, without your knowledge."

"Nay, Merrick. What need had we of an army, when we had the dragon? No man would face such a danger unless driven by a passion as strong as yours." She leaned over him, studying his eyes. "Describe this army of men to me."

"Another time, my love." He gathered her into his arms and pressed his mouth to her temple. "For there's something far more important I must do right now."

But even as he kissed her, he found himself mulling over her words. If the army hadn't been hers, who had sent them? And for what purpose?

To distract her and himself, he began kissing the soft curve of her throat.

She shivered and gave a little laugh. "Careful, my lord. You know where this always leads."

"Aye." He held her a little away. "Are you complaining, my lady? Has a night of loving been too much for you?"

"On the contrary. I'm anticipating more of your clever ministrations."

"You mean this?" He pressed moist kisses across her shoulder, down her collarbone, enjoying the little humming sounds that escaped her throat. "And this?" With his tongue he traced circles around one breast, then the other, until he heard her little gasp of pleasure as his lips closed around one erect nipple.

The heat between them grew. A low flame that was soon a blazing inferno.

And then there were no words as they took each other on another long, slow journey of love.

"Mordred believes I should accept the fact that Hamish might never be free of the fears that imprison his mind." Merrick's fingers played with a strand of Allegra's hair. He loved the way it looked by moonlight, spilling over his arm.

The night was quickly fleeing. Already the first pink ribbons of dawn were curling across the sky.

"Why would Mordred say such a cruel thing?"

"He meant no cruelty, for he loves the lad." Merrick shrugged. "He merely said what others have said. That the blood of the lad's mother flows through him, affecting his mind."

"And what does that imply?"

Merrick's lips thinned. "It is well-known that

Catherine was mad. I've been told that such a thing can carry over into the progeny.''

At his admission, Allegra sat up, hair spilling across her breast. "Is this why no one speaks of Hamish's mother? They believe her mad?"

His tone lowered with passion. "Why else would a woman do the things she did? Almost from the day we wed, she changed from the sweet village lass I'd loved, into someone I hardly recognized. I can't count the number of times she seemed lost somewhere inside her mind, unable to find her way back." He was reminded once again of the pain he'd suffered, watching the disintegration of his wife's health, both in body and mind. "Despite all the changes in her, I wasn't prepared for the end. No sane person would climb to the very edge of the balcony and leap to her death."

"Had she seemed unduly frightened earlier in the night?"

Merrick looked away, his eyes narrowed in thought. "How can I judge? She seemed always frightened of something. A noise in the night could leave her trembling for hours. She saw things no one else saw. Heard things none of us heard. All the signs of madness were there, but I refused to see until it was too late."

Allegra laid a hand over his. "And now you blame yourself for what happened?"

"Aye. I'd been warned to lock her away before she harmed herself or others, but I thought it too cruel. Now my son is without the comfort of his mother."

"He remembers her as a good, loving mother."

He gave a grudging nod of his head. "Though she was often too weary to leave her pallet and tend his needs, she was devoted to the lad."

"And what about her devotion to her husband?"

Merrick flung a hand over his eyes. "Shortly after we wed, she turned away from me. She considered me a barbarian for leaving her alone and going to war. In truth, I was. And still am. But I'll not apologize for driving the invaders from our land."

"Nor should you, Merrick." Allegra caught his hand in hers and lifted it to her lips. "What you do is brave and noble."

He couldn't help smiling at the fierce look in her eyes. "What's this? Are you daring to defend the Sword of the Highlands?"

"Someone must. How can you bear to be so misunderstood?"

"Oh, my little witch." With a chuckle he gathered her into his arms and kissed her long and slow and deep. "Perhaps I should have you ride about the countryside, singing the praises of the lord to his people."

"I would if you but asked, Merrick."

He sat back and studied her through narrowed eyes. "I believe you would, Allegra."

With a sigh he drew her close and kissed her again. This time with a thoroughness that had them both moaning in pleasure. Against her mouth he whispered, "How have I lived for so long without you in my world?"

"And I without you."

He shook his head in amazement. "I believe you mean it."

"I do."

"I don't deserve you, Allegra." He kissed her again, almost reverently. "But I haven't the will to refuse what you offer so freely."

With soft kisses and whispered sighs they led each other into a place where no pain existed. A place that had, from the beginning of time, offered shelter to lovers.

"Good morrow, m'lord." Without warning Mistress MacDonald entered the lord's chambers, trailed by several servants bearing armloads of logs for the fire.

As the fire was stoked and the logs added, Merrick lay on his pallet, one arm beneath his head. Beside him, the furs seemed alive as, with a gasp, Allegra burrowed in and pulled them over her head.

"I checked our Hamish." The old woman walked

around the room, picking up the lord's tunic and cloak and retrieving his boots, which lay against the far wall. "The lad's still sound asleep, m'lord."

"That's good news, Mistress."

Merrick watched as she bent to a second pile of clothing. When she straightened, she was holding a delicate chemise and petticoat, as well as the torn remnants of a gown.

As a serving wench poured fresh water into a basin, the old woman turned to the lord. "Will ye be breaking ye'r fast below stairs this morrow, m'lord? Or would ye prefer to sup here in ye'r chambers?"

"I'll join Hamish and my cousins in the great hall, Mistress."

"Aye, m'lord." She glanced at the mound of furs beside him. "And the healer?"

"I believe she'll join me below stairs."

"As ye wish, m'lord. I'll have Mara prepare the lady's wardrobe…in her chambers." The housekeeper carefully folded the feminine clothes and set them atop a chest before following the servants from the room.

When the door was closed Merrick composed his features before pulling down the furs. "We're alone at last, my lady."

Allegra sat up, shoving hair from her eyes. "Do you think she suspected?"

"Suspected?" He was nearly shaking with the

laughter that threatened. "Whatever are you talking about?"

She shot him a chilling look. "You know exactly what I'm talking about, Merrick. Do you think Mistress MacDonald suspects that I shared your pallet?"

"I doubt that suspect is the correct term." He nodded toward the neat pile of clothing. "The poor dear practically tripped over your chemise and petticoat, which were lying directly in her path."

"Oh, no." Allegra lifted her hands to her cheeks, which were as hot as the fire. "And what of the servants? Did they see, as well?"

"It would have been impossible not to see a lady's intimate garments lying beside the bed. But fear not. I am lord. Though they may whisper, they will say not a word in your presence."

"Oh, don't you see?" She stood and started pacing, too distraught to care that she was naked. "That only makes it worse. Everyone in the fortress will be whispering about us, and laughing behind our backs."

"Whispering, perhaps." He couldn't help grinning at the sight of her, arms crossed over her breasts, walking in circles while wearing nothing but a frown. "There may be some who will be envious, but none, I suspect, who will be laughing."

"How can you make light of this, Merrick?"

"How, my lady?" He got to his feet and held out his hand. "Come here, Allegra."

She stopped her pacing and placed her hand in his. Gently he tugged her across the room until they reached the door, where he reached out and threw the brace.

When he turned to her his smile remained, but there was a smoldering look in his eyes that had her heartbeat speeding up.

"Now there will be no interruptions while I show my gratitude for the gift you gave me all night."

"Merrick..." The words died on her lips as he gathered her close and covered her mouth with his.

Heat poured between them as, on a moan of pleasure, they took each other with all the frenzy of a Highland storm.

Chapter Sixteen

Out of breath, Allegra rushed into her chambers, wearing Merrick's cloak for modesty. As she burst into the room she saw Mara's head come up sharply. A handful of dried herbs fell to the floor before the serving wench turned to face her.

Allegra paused in midstride. "What are you doing, Mara?"

"Merely cleaning up your weeds, as I've been told." The servant nodded toward the tub set in front of a roaring fire. "You'd best hurry and bathe before the water cools."

As Allegra shed the cloak and slipped into the water, the wench approached and began washing her hair.

"Something smells good, Mara. What is it?"

"Mistress MacDonald said I was to use the finest perfumed oils."

Allegra sighed deeply. "How kind of her."

"Not that she had any choice. She said now that you're sharing the lord's bed, we'd all best treat you like a fine lady, or find ourselves begging in the village streets."

Allegra didn't know what hurt more. The words flung with such carelessness, or the fact that the housekeeper would carry such vicious tales. Still, it didn't seem worthy of Mistress MacDonald. She caught the wench's hand, stilling her movements.

Mara's eyes narrowed in challenge. "Do you deny you shared the lord's bed?"

Allegra's voice was pure ice. "I have no further need of your services, Mara. Leave my chamber at once."

"You have to know that if you send me away, the lord will discharge me, and I'll have no place to go."

Allegra almost relented. The plight of the girl touched her tender heart. But when she looked up, she saw not remorse but defiance in Mara's eyes. That only firmed her resolve. "Go now, and I'll say nothing to the lord about this."

"Aye. With pleasure." The girl tossed her head and flounced away, leaving Allegra staring after her.

What had caused such venom? She thought back to the few times she'd been alone with the servant.

Not once had the girl responded to her attempts at kindness.

Allegra sighed as she toweled her hair, then slipped into her gown. She should have expected such treatment. After all, she was the outsider here. Worse, she was feared as a witch. These people had every right to feel protective of their lord.

Still... She paused as she ran a brush through the damp tangles. The servant had gone out of her way to be cruel. The words she'd spoken had been intentionally harsh. As though she'd not only enjoyed them, but had practiced them a time or two for the proper effect.

How many others wanted her banished from Berkshire Castle? She sighed again. The better question would be, were there any here at all who could be counted on as friend?

Before she could despair, she heard her mother's voice, spoken many years ago to her daughters.

There are some in that other world who take pleasure in creating discontent. They pit one against another, sowing the seeds of distrust. They then sit back, enjoying the battle from a safe distance. Beware such people, for they are truly evil.

Allegra decided to reserve judgment on the others in this place. For now she would wait and watch and learn.

* * *

"M'lord. M'lady." As Merrick and Allegra entered the great hall, the housekeeper and servants stood at attention beside a table laden with food.

Merrick acknowledged them with a nod of his head, then held a chair for Allegra.

"Will the lad be joining ye?" The old woman hovered at the lord's elbow.

"Nay, Mistress. He seemed weary this morrow, and asked that Cook fix some gruel."

She nodded. "I'll see to it at once." She poured hot mulled wine and offered the goblets, then looked on as the staff began serving the meal.

Allegra could feel the probing looks as she accepted their offerings. How she wished Hamish were here, to cheer her with his chatter. She'd been so rushed for time, she'd been unable to do more than visit his chambers. But when she'd suggested skipping this meal to remain with the lad, Merrick had insisted she accompany him. He'd even teased her about being unwilling to face the servants' gossip.

And so she sat, head held high, eating in silence, eager for the meal to end.

As Merrick lifted his goblet, Mordred came rushing into the great hall, trailed by Desmond.

"Forgive this intrusion, cousin." Mordred took a moment to catch his breath.

His brother seemed almost giddy with excitement. "You'd best hurry to the village."

"For what purpose?" Merrick looked from one grave expression to the other. "Invaders?"

"Aye." Mordred could barely control his agitation. "It would appear they attacked in the night, burning several huts that lay just outside the village."

"So close?" Merrick turned to Allegra. "You'll stay with the lad?"

"Of course."

He closed a hand over hers. "You'll stay close to the castle until I return."

She nodded. "I understand." She could see the housekeeper staring at their joined hands with a frown, and Mara's words came back to her. "I'll go now and comfort him."

Merrick was on his feet at once, holding her chair as she stood. "I'll walk with you, Allegra." He turned to the housekeeper. "Ask a stable lad to see that my horse is saddled, Mistress."

"Aye, m'lord."

He turned to his cousins. "You'll ride with me?"

"Nay." Mordred shook his head. "Desmond and I thought it wise to carry the warning to nearby villages while you survey the damage."

Merrick nodded his approval before striding from the room.

As Allegra moved by Merrick's side, she gave a

soft sigh. "How bold of the invaders to strike so close to the Sword of the Highlands."

"Perhaps they've heard the rumors that he has been bewitched by a beautiful lady." He looked down at her with a gentle smile. "I warned you, my love. There are no secrets in Berkshire Castle."

At his words she went very still.

He turned to glance at her. "What is it?"

"Nothing." She composed her features and continued walking beside him. But as she climbed the stairs the thought persisted. If there were no secrets, then surely some here at Berkshire Castle knew what had happened to Merrick's wife.

Now, while she was to be left on her own, she must devise a way to pry their secrets from these people.

"Good morrow, Hamish." Allegra hurried into the lad's chambers and found him sitting by the fire, spooning gruel sweetened with honey into his mouth. "Your father has gone to the village." She sat beside him on the chaise. "Are you feeling strong enough for a walk in the garden after you've eaten?"

The boy nodded without much enthusiasm.

Alarmed, Allegra touched a hand to his forehead. He seemed much more frail than he had only an hour earlier when she'd left to break her fast.

Though there was no fever, his skin seemed unusually pale, his eyes dull.

"What's wrong, Hamish?"

The boy shrugged. "I know not. I took the potion you sent me, but it didn't help."

"The potion?" Though her eyes went wide, she fought to keep the fear from her voice, so as not to alarm the lad.

He nodded. "Mara brought it just as I awakened, and said I was to take it before eating anything." He wrinkled his nose. "It tasted so foul, I could barely swallow it. But Mara said you'd be angry with me if I didn't take all of it."

"Oh, Hamish." Allegra drew him close and pressed her cheek to the top of his head. "Did Mara bring you the gruel, as well?"

"Aye."

She took the bowl from his hand. "You mustn't finish this."

"Why?"

"Because it will only make you weaker." She crossed the room, then paused in the doorway. "I'll be back within a few minutes with something that will help."

Once in her room, Allegra worked quickly to crush the leaves of pennyroyal, then steeped them in a goblet of hot water and milk thistle. By the time she'd returned to Hamish's chambers, the tea had cooled enough to drink.

She handed him the goblet. "You must drink all, until it's empty."

When he did as she ordered, she took the empty cup from his hands and drew him close once more. Keeping her tone level, she said, "It will take a while for the tea to work its magic. When it does, you'll feel your strength slowly return."

She drew in a calming breath, then tipped up his face until he met her eyes. "I want you to promise me something, Hamish."

He looked at her with such trust it was almost frightening. She resolved to do all in her power to keep this lad safe.

"From now on, you're to take nothing unless it comes from my hands. Can you do that?"

"But why?"

She forced herself to smile. "It's part of the magic. I must touch it before you do. If anyone else touches it, the chain of magic will be broken."

He brightened and clapped his hands with excitement. "In order for the magic to work, it must come from your hands to mine?"

"Exactly so. And one more thing, Hamish. No one must know about this except us. Do you agree?"

"Aye."

As he sat back, she could see his strength return-ing, along with the color in his cheeks. She was grateful that the potion given him by Mara hadn't had time to take effect before the tea worked its magic.

She deeply regretted deception. But the lad was too young to understand that someone wanted him harmed. Besides, Allegra had no way of knowing if Mara was alone in this villainy, or if there were others. She knew this much. She would have to work quickly to uncover the truth. The lad's very life depended on it. For somehow, he was key to this mystery.

He caught her hand, breaking through her thoughts. "Can we walk in the garden now?"

She nodded. "Aye. I believe the sunshine would be good for both of us." And would clear her mind for whatever lay ahead.

As they passed Mara and several other servants, Allegra saw the serving wench's head come up sharply. She merely smiled and continued walking, her arm firmly around the lad's shoulders.

As they stepped into the sunshine, Allegra breathed deeply and led Hamish along a grassy path until they came to a stone bench near a fountain. "We'll sit here and rest a bit before going on."

As they settled themselves, Allegra closed her eyes and concentrated on her family. Her mother at her loom. Her grandmother working the garden in Allegra's absence. Kylia splashing in a stream, since she loved the water. And Gwenellen off in the forest, chasing fairies on her winged horse.

A sense of peace came over her.

Hamish tugged on her arm. "Why are you smiling?"

She opened her eyes. "I was thinking of my family, and that always makes me smile." She had a sudden thought. "Tell me about your mother."

The boy's face grew animated. "She was very beautiful. Her hair looked like spun gold. Her eyes were as blue as the sky. And when she smiled, I felt safe."

"I know the feeling." Allegra brushed at a wisp of hair that was caught by the breeze.

Hamish's smiled faded. "She often couldn't get out of bed. And when she did, she would do strange things."

"Such as?"

He thought a moment. "She once accused a servant of stealing the circlet of gold that Father gave her when they wed. But when Father searched, he found the trinket in the bedcovers and ordered her to apologize to the servant."

"Was the servant Mara?"

The little boy's eyes widened. "Aye. How did you know?"

Allegra said softly, "Just a thought. What other strange things did your mother do?"

"She would fall asleep at table while we supped. She fell down the stairs and said she'd been pushed, though no one was near when it happened. One night she ran into the garden tearing at her clothes and saying they were burning her flesh."

Allegra thought about all the treasures that grew in the meadows and forests. For every one that healed, there was another that, in the wrong hands, could cause great pain. A healer who chose evil over good could do great harm with such knowledge. "What did your father do?"

"He went after her and ordered her to come inside at once. And when she did, she locked herself in her chambers and refused to come out for days."

Allegra's tone softened. "It must have pained you and your father to see these changes in your beautiful mother. What did you do, Hamish?"

"I hid." His voice fell to a whisper. "I used to hide a lot."

"Where did you hide?"

"In my secret place."

"Can you share it with me?"

He took a moment before nodding. "I found a little passageway tucked into a wall in my chambers. I discovered that if I remained very quiet, no one could find me there." As an afterthought he added,

"While I was there, I could hear everything that was said in my mother's rooms."

Allegra's heart began beating overtime. "What did you learn while hiding there, Hamish?"

The little boy fell silent, watching the flight of a butterfly. When at last he turned back to her his eyes were blank.

Very gently Allegra repeated her question, all the while watching his eyes. "What did you overhear while you were hiding, Hamish?"

He shook his head. "I can't recall."

She could tell, by the way his eyes remained vacant, that he was telling the truth. Whatever he'd overheard, it was now buried deep inside his mind. But why? Because whatever had happened to his mother on her last night was too terrible to recall? Or because the truth might condemn the father he adored?

Allegra's mind simply refused to accept that. But she knew, deep in her heart, that her love for Merrick MacAndrew could be blinding her to the possibility that he'd had a hand in his wife's death.

As painful as the truth might prove to be, she had a right to know. As did the others.

She had earned Hamish's trust. Now she must learn the secrets locked in some small corner of his mind, no matter who might be harmed in the process.

Chapter Seventeen

"Mistress MacDonald." Allegra saw the startled look that came into the old woman's eyes.

"What're ye doing in the scullery?" The housekeeper backed away. "Ye shouldn't be here. 'Tisn't a fit place for the likes of ye."

"The likes of me? What does that mean?"

"Just..." The old woman glanced around nervously, to assure herself that they were alone. "Now that ye're so special to the lord, ye shouldn't be seen in the scullery."

"I'm the same person I was yesterday."

"If ye think that, lass, ye're a fool. The lord's lady doesn't mingle with the servants." Eyes as sharp as a blackbird's peered into hers. "Why did ye come down here?"

"To ask you a question."

"Ask, then. I've work to see to."

"How long has Mara been a servant here in Berkshire Castle?"

"Mara?" The old woman thought a moment. "Four years now. Since she lost her parents. The lady Catherine was quite taken with her and asked the lord to invite her to live at the castle, as he has with so many who have no home. It's always been his way."

"Did Mara grow up in the village?"

"Aye."

"Does she return there, to visit with friends?"

The housekeeper shook her head. "Not that I know of. She prefers life here in the castle."

Allegra started away, then as an afterthought turned. "Were her parents killed by the invaders?"

Mistress MacDonald chewed her lip. "As I recall, they died in their beds. Some said they were cursed. Others thought they'd eaten rancid meat. Whatever the reason, they went off to their beds one night and were found dead the next morning. It is the reason I put up with the lazy wench, for I realize she has no other family."

"And what of Mara? Did she eat what her parents ate? Was she sick? How did she escape the curse?"

The old woman shrugged. "I don't recall. Ye can ask her yerself."

"Aye. Thank you, Mistress. I shall."

As she turned away the housekeeper cleared her throat. "M'lady. Hold a moment."

Allegra turned. The old woman's tone softened. "It gladdens my heart to see that ye and the lord have found…comfort in each other. He's been alone far too long. And though ye're not like us, I've seen a goodness in ye. Ye've brought laughter into the lad's life. And love into the lord's." She looked down at her hands, as though aware she'd over-stepped her bounds and said far too much. "Go now. I've work to see to."

"Aye. Thank you, Mistress MacDonald." Allegra could have hugged the old dear for those words, but she knew if she did, she would cause the house-keeper discomfort.

Her heart was pounding as she hurried up the stairs to Hamish's chambers, determined not to leave him alone again. Though she'd found a friend in the housekeeper, she knew in her heart that the serving girl Mara was a dangerous adversary.

As she stepped through the doorway she saw Mara just flouncing out. The servant shot Allegra a dark look before descending the stairs.

"Hamish." Allegra hurried across the room. "Did Mara give you anything to eat?"

He looked up with a smile. "She said you'd sent me some tea. I told her I wouldn't take it from her hands. She said she would tell my father that I've been disrespectful. I don't believe she likes our game, my lady.''

Allegra gave him a hard, quick hug. ''Perhaps not. But I'm delighted that you remembered the rules. Now.'' She looked around. ''While no one is here, why don't you show me your hiding place?''

With a delighted laugh he led her to a spot beside the hearth, where he touched a hand to the stone. At once a crack in the wall opened, revealing a narrow passageway.

As they stepped inside, he touched another stone, causing the crack to close. Allegra was forced to hunch over to keep from bumping her head. Ahead of her, little Hamish inched along until he pointed to a pinprick of light up ahead. Soon the light grew and she could see that they'd reached Catherine's chambers.

There was no doorway on this end. Only a narrow crevice that permitted a limited view of the space between the bed and a side table. As they huddled together, they saw Mara enter the chambers. With a furtive glance around, the servant began stripping the pallet, carrying the furs to the balcony to shake them before returning them to the bed.

But why? Allegra wondered. These chambers had been vacant for more than a year now. What could the servant hope to uncover at this late date?

Each time Mara passed between the bed and side

table, Allegra was able to catch a quick glimpse of her before she disappeared again. But every sound could be heard clearly. The snap of the bed linens as she shook them over the balcony. The tap of her booted feet on the wooden floor. The gurgle of water being poured from a pitcher into a basin. And finally the closing of the door as, satisfied that the room had been thoroughly cleaned, the servant took her leave.

When Allegra turned to Hamish, she saw that his face had drained of all color. "What is it, lad? What do you recall?"

"Mara." His voice was little more than a whisper.

"Go on." Allegra dropped to her knees and gathered him close. "What about Mara?"

"As Mama's maid she was always in her chambers. That night..." His tone lowered. "The night my mama died, Mara brought broth. When Mama wouldn't take it, Mara held the spoon to her lips and forced her."

Allegra closed her eyes a moment. "It's as I thought. Come, Hamish. As soon as your father returns from the village, we must tell him what you recall."

She slowly made her way from the hiding place.

After Hamish touched a finger to the stone, causing the space to open, they stepped into his room.

Allegra straightened. Feeling a chill pass through her, she turned and felt a rush of alarm when she spotted Mordred and Desmond standing with their backs to the closed door. On their faces were matching looks of something she couldn't quite discern.

"What is it?" She started toward them. "Has something happened to Merrick?"

"Not yet." Mordred took a step closer. "But soon, I pray."

At his strange words Allegra stepped back, shielding Hamish with her body. "What do you mean? What do you want here?"

Mordred crossed his arms over his chest and regarded her with a grim smile. "It's fortunate that you didn't think to brace the lad's door, as you've been bracing your own."

"It was you outside my chambers." And all the while she'd believed it to be Mara.

Mordred shot a sideways glance at his brother. "We'd hoped to frighten you enough to send you fleeing into the night. And would have, if you hadn't barred our way."

"Is that what you did to the lord's wife?"

"She was so much simpler. Such a trusting little fool. With Merrick distracted by invasions on our borders, we had little trouble with the lady Catherine. Especially since her maid had been picked by her and—" he gave a cruel laugh "—trained by us." He glanced at the lad, peering from behind Allegra's skirts. "The boy would have been an easy matter to dispose of as well, if you hadn't come along when you did."

"Mara's potions." Allegra dropped a hand on the lad's shoulder. "Your bold, sunny nature was slowly being eroded, as was your mind." She turned back to Mordred. "Why?" She studied these two men, who could have been mistaken for brave Highland warriors. "Why did you wish to harm a helpless woman and her son?"

"It had nothing to do with them. They were simply the means to an end."

Allegra could feel the evil all around her. Alive. Pulsing with darkness. As she looked at these two men, she saw it in their eyes. And suddenly she understood.

"This is about Merrick. You hate him. Not only because he is a powerful lord, but because of his goodness."

"Goodness." Mordred sneered. "It's that goodness that will bring him down."

"I don't understand." Allegra looked from one man to the other.

Mordred gave a sly grin. "Our cousin thinks, because he has shared hearth and home with us, that we are his loyal subjects. After all, we've fought by his side. And even offered comfort while he grieved for his beloved Catherine.''

Allegra reached out, taking Hamish's trembling hand in hers. ''And all the while you plotted and schemed against him.''

''We had to, since he wouldn't accommodate us by dying in battle. The man seems charmed. No matter how many swords he faces, he manages to evade death. Even the army we ordered to greet him at the border of the Mystical Kingdom couldn't defeat him.''

''It was you who sent those warriors.''

''Aye.'' Mordred withdrew a small, sharp dirk from his waist and advanced on Allegra. ''Now, my lady, you and the lad will come with us.''

''Where?''

''You'll see.''

She lifted her head. ''I'll go anywhere you say, as long as you promise to leave Hamish here.''

''Aye. I'll leave him here. Of course, I'll have to slit his throat first, to insure his silence. Is that what you want?'' He made a grab for the boy, and Allegra leaped in front of him, barring his way.

''You'll have to kill me first.''

He gave a cruel laugh. ''As you wish.''

He slashed out with the knife, catching her arm as she stepped back. She gave a hiss of pain and closed a hand over the wound to stem the flow of blood. When he lunged again, she ducked aside, and his blade bit deeply into the wall beside her head.

While he struggled to withdraw his knife, she caught the lad's hand and started across the room, hoping to make it to the door. Before she could open it, Hamish was snatched from her grasp.

When she turned, Desmond was holding the boy in his arms, with the blade of his knife pressed to his tender flesh.

Allegra froze.

"Now, my lady." Mordred gave a mock bow before closing a hand around her wrist. "You will do our bidding, or the lad will pay."

"Will you toss me from the balcony, as you did Catherine?"

His eyes narrowed. "That wouldn't be wise. I doubt the household would believe such a thing of you. They might have, if Mara had been able to force her potions on you." He glanced at his brother. "I've decided that the death of you and the lad must be much more dramatic. You'll be found in a meadow, your poor mangled bodies bloodied by the swords of barbarian invaders."

"You seem sure of yourself. How will you lure the barbarians to that very place?"

Mordred laughed and his brother joined him. "Right now Merrick is viewing the charred remains of several huts just beyond the village, which were attacked and burned last night by…invaders. Sadly, there were none who survived.''

''You and your brother saw to that, I suppose.''

''Aye. It was unfortunate, since we were forced to sacrifice our own people. But we needed someone to blame for the deaths of you and the lad. What better idea than invaders who attack and then retreat?''

''How will you explain Merrick's death?''

''As lover and father, he can be counted on to come to your aid, especially when he finds this missive.''

Mordred reached inside his tunic and retrieved a scrolled parchment. ''When he arrives at the meadow he will share your fate at the hands of one remaining invader, who will, of course, escape before we can punish him for his crime.'' Mordred laughed. ''The people will rise up in anger and unite behind me, their new leader.''

His smile faded, replaced with a look so frightening, Allegra wanted to shrink from him. ''Now, woman, you will walk with us to the garden, and from there to the meadow. If you should cry out or do anything to draw attention to yourself, my brother will kill the lad.'' He twisted her arm until she gasped in pain. ''Do you understand me?''

She nodded, unable to speak over the hard knot

of fear lodged in her throat, for she had no doubt these two were capable of all they threatened.

"Good." He smiled, though it never reached his eyes. They were, she realized, lifeless. Dead. The evil inside him had drained all the light from his eyes, reflecting the darkness of his soul.

He linked his arm with hers. Pressed to her side, hidden by his sleeve, was a small, sharp dirk. "You and the lad will be the perfect tool to aid in the final destruction of our dear cousin, Merrick."

As they passed Mara, Allegra saw the girl nod her head, as though in silent understanding. The servant was aware of whatever these two evil men planned.

For now, with Hamish's life in jeopardy, she was helpless to stop them. But when they reached their destination, she was determined to find a way to fight them. Though the depth of their evil frightened her, she knew she must confront it.

As she walked beside Mordred, she reached out a hand to Hamish and felt the way he was trembling.

Her heart went out to this poor lad. For one made timid and shy by evil potions, this must seem like a nightmare. But for now, there was little she could do to comfort him, except to try, with every fiber of her being, to give him her love and strength.

"Courage, Hamish. You mustn't lose heart."

At her words, Mordred gave a chilling laugh.

"Nay, lad. Don't lose heart. Let us take it from you and feed it to the forest creatures."

He leaned close, and she saw the way the boy shrank from him. Whatever kindness he'd once shown the boy was now gone. In its place were his true feelings of cruelty beyond belief.

Determined to spare the lad any further pain, Allegra stopped in her tracks and turned to face Mordred. "Unless you agree to stop tormenting this boy, I'll shout down the entire household, and you may kill me where I stand."

Mordred's eyes narrowed. "I'll do better than that. I warned you, woman." To his brother he said, "Slit the lad's throat."

"Nay!" Allegra caught hold of Desmond's hand. "Please, I beg of you. If you'll spare the lad, I'll go quietly."

"This is your last chance." Mordred gave her a shove as they stepped out into the garden. "You'll walk quietly to the meadow, or have the lad's blood on your hands."

It occurred to Allegra as they moved woodenly along the grassy path that the day was too beautiful. How could the sun be shining? How could the flowers be so fragrant? Even the chorus of birdsong seemed to mock her.

Oh, Mama. Oh, Gram. Help me find within myself the courage needed to deal with this evil.

Almost at once she felt a sense of peace.

She glanced over at Hamish, being carried in Desmond's arms. His little face tearstained. His eyes closed against the coming danger.

She would save the lad, she vowed. Or die trying.

Chapter Eighteen

Merrick urged his steed toward the fortress. The viciousness of the attack against his own villagers had left him stunned and reeling. The invaders had been cunning and cruel, first setting fire to the huts, and then killing entire families as they fled the flames. None had been spared, down to the smallest infant held in its mother's arms.

The men had apparently been killed quickly, dropped by arrows from a longbow as they fled the flames. The women and young lasses had suffered a harsher fate, having been brutalized and tortured before going to their deaths.

What sort of barbarians could do such things? The first rule of warfare he'd learned as a lad had been to spare those not directly involved in the conflict. Yet these had been peaceful villagers, asleep in their homes, slaughtered like sheep.

He was grateful that he'd asked Allegra to stay close to Hamish. The lad had become so fragile, Merrick feared for him. The boy was bound to hear talk by the servants about this barbarism. Would it remind him of the cruel death of his own mother? Merrick pushed aside the nagging thought that, if pushed too far, his fearful son might leap to his death the way Catherine had.

As he reached the courtyard of Berkshire Castle, he dismounted and handed over the reins to a stable lad before hurrying inside.

Upstairs he made his way to his son's chambers, needing to hold him for just a moment. The images of the villagers would stay in his mind for a very long time. Just having Hamish close to his heart would ease the pain.

He opened the door and looked around in surprise. Instead of the tidy pallet with its carefully folded furs, the bed was in disarray, as was the room. There was a gap in the wall near the hearth. What was this? A passageway? After peering inside, he realized it led to his wife's chambers. Puzzled, he stepped back, wondering why Hamish had never mentioned this. Perhaps he had only today discovered it.

Turning away, Merrick spied the parchment lying on the lad's pallet. As he unrolled it, the words had his heart stopping.

We have the lad and witch. Come to the meadow alone, or they die.

Who had Allegra and Hamish? And why? Invaders couldn't have penetrated this fortress.

As he started toward the door he spotted the blood on the floor.

Blood?

He knelt and touched a finger to the droplet, feeling his heart sink like a stone. The thought of his son or Allegra being harmed had him filled with helpless fury. With a muttered oath he stormed down the hallway to Allegra's chambers and saw the serving wench, dressed in one of Allegra's gowns, studying herself in the looking glass.

"Mara." His brows drew together in a furious scowl. "What are you doing?"

The lass took a step back, her hand at her throat. "I...meant no harm. I just wanted to see how I would look in something so fine."

"By what right do you dare to touch the lady's things?" Merrick's fingers closed around her upper arm. Through gritted teeth he snarled, "You'll tell me what this is about, or I swear by heaven I'll kill you where you stand."

"It wasn't my doing." Tears sprang to her eyes. "Mordred promised me I'd be lady of the castle when he became lord."

"Mordred?" Merrick's eyes narrowed as he released her and took a step back. "This is my cousin's doing?"

"Aye." She rubbed her tender arm and lifted her head, enjoying the fact that she'd managed to catch the lord by surprise. Perhaps he wasn't as all-knowing as his people believed him to be. "You're too late to stop him. By now the lad and his healer are dead."

"Nay." He swung away and raced down the stairs, sword in hand.

By the time he'd reached the garden, the fear and shock had turned to blind, searing fury. Though he had no idea yet what this was about, he knew this. He would find Allegra and Hamish before it was too late, or those who harmed them would never live to see another day. For if he didn't make it in time, his own life would never again have purpose or meaning.

With Mordred firmly in control, their little party had left the garden of Berkshire Castle behind, and had entered a high meadow abloom with heather. While they walked Allegra's mind was awhirl with possibilities. If she could distract their abductors, she could snatch Hamish from Desmond's arms and try to flee. But here in the meadow, there was no place to hide. It was useless to try to run. Instead, they would have to stand and fight. But how? They had no weapons with which to defend themselves.

"This will do." Mordred released his hold on her arm and stepped away, taking his sword from its scabbard.

In the same instant Desmond lowered Hamish to the ground. At once the lad stumbled toward Allegra and fell weeping into her arms.

She gathered him close and pressed her mouth to his temple. "You must be brave, Hamish."

"I'm afraid." He wrapped his chubby arms around her neck and burrowed his face into her shoulder. "Why would Father's cousins wish to harm us?"

"Why, lad?" Mordred's voice had them both looking up. "I'll tell you why. Desmond and I have been partaking of the crumbs of your father's kindness for a lifetime."

Beside him, Desmond nodded in agreement. It occurred to Allegra that Desmond took all his orders from his older brother. In fact, she wondered if he'd ever had a single thought that hadn't been directed by Mordred.

"Why should Merrick MacAndrew live in a great castle, while our own cottage lay in ruins?" Mordred's tone lowered with anger. "And why, since we all apprenticed as warriors together, should Merrick be made lord over us?"

Allegra's eyes widened. ''I see. So it is jealousy that rules you. Why do you think the people of Berkshire chose Merrick as their lord?''

''Because his father was lord before him.''

''Nay, Mordred. That is the way of the English. But here in Scotland, the title lord cannot be inherited. Here, every man must earn his own reward. And his own respect.'' She turned to the boy. ''Remember this, Hamish. The people sensed in your father the ability to lead them through good times and bad. The title lord is an honor bestowed on him not only because of his prowess as a warrior, but also because of his goodness and fairness as a leader.''

''What of Father's cousins?'' the boy asked softly. ''Why could they not be lord?''

''Because they were unworthy. You see, they're possessed by evil.''

''You dare to call us evil, witch?'' Mordred advanced on her and swung his hand in an arc, slapping her with such force, her head snapped to one side and stars danced before her eyes.

''Don't hurt her.'' In his anguish, Hamish forgot his fears and caught Mordred's fist before he could use it on her again.

Alarmed, Desmond pulled a knife from his waist and raised it over the boy.

''Nay, Desmond.'' Mordred lifted a hand to fend

off his brother before he could carry out his intention. "We need them alive for a little while longer."

"The witch called us evil."

Mordred laughed. "And so we are." He nodded in satisfaction as Desmond returned his dirk to his waist. "You see, the witch and the lad are merely the bait to trap our real enemy into coming here, where he'll be helpless. When we've finished with our cousin, I'll give you the pleasure of killing these two." He glanced at Allegra, who had gathered Hamish into her arms. "My brother enjoys killing. Don't you, Desmond?"

The younger man nodded. "Mordred used to let me kill animals, just for the pleasure it brought me."

Allegra felt a chill race along her spine and close like an icy fist around her heart.

"I taught him to hunt, so he could enjoy the sport of killing." Mordred looked up, then nodded toward the distant ridge. "See? Even now our latest prey is almost here, Desmond. Then the hunt will be truly over."

Merrick raced through the gardens, past the edge of the meadow where Allegra and Hamish had planted their herb garden. The wattle fence, so carefully woven of sticks and willow branches, was a shocking reminder of the love that had been lavished on this place.

Love. His heart contracted with pain at the thought. He'd willingly have given his life for that of his son. And the same was true of the gentle witch. He loved her as he'd never believed he could love anyone. And because of him, her life, which had once been idyllic, might now end in violence.

The thought had him racing through the fields of heather until his lungs burned from the effort. As he came up over a ridge, he saw the figures in the distance and charged toward them, praying he wasn't too late.

"So, cousin. You found our missive."

Mordred and Desmond formed a united front, standing with weapons lifted as Merrick came to a sudden halt.

"Allegra. Hamish." He stared beyond the men to where the woman stood, holding the lad in her arms. "I saw blood. Have you been harmed?"

Allegra shook her head. "It's of no consequence. It was a small cut."

Mordred advanced. "Drop your sword, cousin. Or my brother will slit the lad's throat."

"Nay, Merrick. Don't leave yourself defenseless," Allegra shouted into the stillness that seemed to have descended on the meadow. Not a breath of air stirred. Not a single blossom moved. "For no matter what you do, they intend to kill us."

Allegra's words were ignored as Merrick tossed his weapon aside. "Do with me what you will. But I implore you to spare these innocents."

"And let them tell the villagers what we did here?" Mordred threw back his head and laughed. "You must all die this day, cousin."

With all his strength he thrust his sword, and Merrick leaped aside, dodging the full impact. Instead, the blade of Mordred's sword slammed into his shoulder, causing him to suck in a breath at the searing pain as his cousin stepped closer and cruelly plucked his weapon free.

Hamish cried out when he saw his father drop to his knees, blood streaming from his wound.

"You won't fare as well with my brother, for his aim is true." Mordred motioned for Desmond to attack. "Now you can have your pleasure, Desmond."

The younger man started toward Merrick, lifting his sword high.

As Merrick struggled to face his opponent, Allegra concentrated all her energy until the hilt of the sword began to glow like the sun. With a cry of pain Desmond dropped his weapon before clasping his burned hand to his chest.

Mordred caught his brother by the shoulder. "What is it, Desmond?"

The younger man looked around wildly. "It must

be the witch. She's used her magic against me. Kill her quickly, before she bewitches us both.''

Mordred gave a chilling laugh. ''Never fear, Desmond. Before we're through with the witch, she'll beg us to kill her. As will her lover.''

He snagged a handful of her hair and pulled her close. ''But first, we'll make her watch her lover die, ever so slowly.''

''Release the woman.'' Despite his pain Merrick stumbled to his feet and started toward them.

''Stop him, Desmond.''

At Mordred's words, the younger man took the knife from his waist and tossed it, watching as it landed with a dull thud in Merrick's chest. As the color slowly drained from Merrick's face, his hands closed around the hilt of the weapon, buried deep in his flesh, but the pain was too great to budge it. With a look of surprise mingled with pain, he dropped to his knees.

''Now, witch.'' Mordred watched as Merrick struggled for his very life. ''Before death claims my dear cousin, Desmond and I will show you what we did to the lovely lasses who were routed from their beds last night by our fire. Though it will pleasure us greatly, it should add to Merrick's pain considerably. I want him to die watching the woman he loves being humiliated at the hands of those he trusted.''

Allegra was repulsed by the touch of these men. But though she vaguely heard the mocking laughter as the two brothers began to tear at her clothes, the only thing that seemed to penetrate her consciousness was the sobbing of the lad who knelt in the grass and clutched at his father's hands. She knew in that instant that she would do whatever it took to save them all from these madmen. Even if she were forced to pay the greatest price of all.

Mara came racing up. As she struggled for breath she gazed down at Merrick. "Is he dead, then?"

"Nay." Mordred laughed. "But soon. We're about to add to his pain."

Allegra used that moment of distraction to gather her thoughts. She stood facing the enemy, looking regal in nothing more than a tattered gown that, though shredded, was still attached at both cuffs, displaying bits of flesh barely concealed by a delicate chemise and petticoats. "Tell me, Mordred," she asked. "What will you do when we are all dead?"

"I shall be lord." He made a grand sweep of his hand. "And all this will belong to me."

Allegra glanced at Mara. "Have you promised to make her your lady?"

"Aye," the wench boasted. "And I shall have all the lovely gowns that were once yours."

"Fool." Mordred swung his hand in an arc, slap-

ping her across the face with enough force to cause
her to drop to her knees. "Did you really think I
would take a lowly servant as lady of the castle?"

The girl brushed a hand across her mouth and
stared at the blood in astonishment. "You promised.
I killed my parents for you, so that I'd be invited to
live at the castle and earn the trust of the lord and
his family. I helped you kill his lady, and stole the
lad's mind with my potions."

"You did a fine job, Mara. You've earned your
reward." Without a flicker of emotion Mordred
drew back his arm and plunged his sword into her
chest, then calmly withdrew the bloody weapon and
thrust it into a clump of heather at his feet.

Ignoring the whimpers from Hamish, he turned to
Allegra with a sneer. "You won't be as fortunate,
witch. Instead of a quick death, I'll see that you
suffer first."

Allegra continued to face him without flinching.
"And what of your brother? What role will he play
in your reign? Or will you be forced to kill him, as
well, so that there is no need to share the rewards
of your evil deeds?"

Desmond's brows shot up. It was obvious that
he'd never given a thought to his own future. He
turned to his brother. "How do you answer the
witch?"

"Never fear, Desmond. You'll be my man-at-arms, and share in all the wealth and comfort of Berkshire Castle.''

Desmond spoke with the petulant voice of a child. ''But I'll not be lord.''

''Of course not. I'm the eldest. Besides, you'd have never thought of this on your own. Without me, you'd still be living in that hovel in the forest.''

''I loved that cottage.'' His vacant eyes lit with the memory. ''Do you remember how our mother welcomed us home from our first battle with fresh scones and hot mulled wine? And wept with us over the loss of our father?''

''Aye. And would have consoled us over the harsh winter with her hugs and kisses until the lot of us were frozen and half-starved, if I hadn't seen a better way.''

''A better way?'' Desmond stared blankly at his brother. ''I don't understand.''

''You've never understood. It's always been up to me to figure a way for us to survive. I knew that Merrick's mother took in all those who were orphaned. And so she did with us, when our poor mother met her...untimely death.''

Allegra stared at the man in stunned disbelief. Even though she knew him to be a cold-blooded killer, this was beyond anything she could imagine. ''Are you saying you killed your own mother, Mordred, in order to live in Berkshire Castle?''

"And why not? I spared her a slow death by starvation. And my brother and I were soon living like lords."

He was laughing when Desmond rose up with a roar of pain and brought his fist to his face. "Nay. Not our mother. She loved us. Loved me especially, as no one else ever had."

"Aye." Shocked and angered, Mordred mopped at the blood that poured from his nose. "Our mother was the only woman who could ever love you, you fool."

Before he could say more, Desmond came at him, head first, and drove him backward with such force, he landed on his back in the heather. Then the slow-witted man was on him, fighting like a feral dog, battering his older brother almost senseless.

Without warning, Desmond felt the sudden sharp sting of a dirk buried deep beneath his breastbone. For a moment the younger man seemed too stunned to react. Then he stiffened before slumping over.

Mordred pushed the body of his brother aside and struggled to his feet, his breathing tortured and ragged. Then he turned the full force of his fury on Allegra, who had used the distraction to hurry to Merrick's side.

"Desmond was a simpleton. Without your interference, he would have gladly served beside me in any capacity I chose. But you had to put ideas in his mind. It's your fault I was forced to kill him. Now, witch, you'll pay for this.''

"Nay." As he reached for Allegra, a childish voice stopped him.

He turned with a smile. "What, Hamish? Has our cowardly little lad found his courage?"

"Aye." The boy stood facing him, his little body trembling as he began speaking, not to Mordred, but to the vision that hovered nearby. "I remember now, Mama. I remember everything."

Allegra turned and saw the beautiful golden-haired woman smiling at her son, her arms out-stretched as though to embrace him.

Hamish's voice grew stronger. "I remember the way Mordred and Desmond came into your chambers after Mara forced you to swallow the broth. I remember the sound of their laughter as they tossed you over the balcony. I first remembered it the day I was climbing the tree in the meadow. Mara had given me a tea to drink, saying it would give me wings to fly. Instead it brought all the memories back, and when I fell, I fled in fear. Then I forgot again. But now I remember everything."

The woman seemed to shimmer and glow as, weeping, she drew near and gathered her son into her arms, pressing a kiss to his cheek. Then she turned and touched a hand to Allegra's shoulder before the light around her grew so bright, it was impossible to look at her.

Allegra covered her eyes and turned away. When she lifted her head the woman was gone, but the warmth of her touch remained like a blessing.

Mordred turned away from the boy with an air of dismissal. "How could you know such things? You weren't even there the night your mother died."

"I was hiding in the passageway. I saw and heard everything."

"Then why did you never speak of it?"

"It was stolen from my mind. Mara came to my chambers and gave me a potion to calm me. Perhaps that's why I forgot. Perhaps that's when I lost my courage, as well. Whatever the reason, I remember it now. And I no longer fear you. You killed my mother." Hamish ran at him. "But you'll not kill again."

Mordred's arm shot out to stop him. Instead, the lad sank his teeth into the man's flesh until he let out a howl of fury. When Mordred managed to shake him free, he reached for his sword, only to find Allegra already there, holding it in her hands.

A sly smile twisted his mouth. "What will you do with that, witch? You're barely big enough to hold it in both hands. How do you hope to wield it as a weapon?"

"You're right, of course." She flung it aside and

stood facing him. "I have no need of such a puny weapon. You are filled with evil, Mordred, and there is but one force stronger."

"You think yourself stronger than me, witch?" He reached for her, and was startled when his hands refused to close. Instead his fingers felt so heavy he could barely move them. His legs, too, refused to move. He stood frozen to the spot as Allegra lifted her arms high and began to chant.

Her voice had an eerie quality that had him going completely still, suspended in place. Even the meadow seemed frozen in time. No insects buzzed. No birds sang. Not a hint of breeze rippled the heather.

"Mighty one, reach out your hand. Remove this evil from our land."

Though there wasn't a single cloud in the sky, a bolt of lightning shot from the heavens, knocking Mordred to the ground. He lay there writhing and moaning while his flesh, and then his bones, began to slowly burn away until there was nothing left of him but a cloud of dark, acrid smoke. At last there was a crash of thunder that echoed across the hills. As the sound faded, the smoke dissipated.

This display of magic had drained Allegra. It took all her energy just to drop to her knees beside Merrick. The gaping wound in his chest flowed with a river of blood, until the ground beneath him ran red with it. His eyes were closed, his body as still as death.

The little boy caught his father's hands in his, and looked over at Allegra. "Save him, healer."

"If only I could. Oh, Hamish, if only I could." She knelt beside him, unable to do more than shake her head.

The silence was broken only by the sounds of the boy's sobs as he struggled to hold tightly to the man he loved more than life itself.

Chapter Nineteen

"Please, healer." Hamish leaned over his father's still figure, unmindful of the tears that fell, mingling with Merrick's blood. "Do something. Help him."

So much blood, Allegra thought. It took all her effort to touch a finger to Merrick's temple, searching for some connection to this man who owned her heart. She could feel nothing. No pain. No confusion. No thoughts of any kind. Just a stillness that had her absolutely terrified.

She had already been drained of all her power, dealing with the evil one. She was completely helpless to save the man she loved.

Desperate, she lifted her face to the heavens and shouted, "Mum. Gram. Please. Oh, please come. I need you so."

Hamish watched as the last of the color seemed to drain from Merrick's flesh, leaving his face as pale and cool as though carved from granite.

"He's dead, isn't he? Just like Mama."

"Nay." Because she couldn't accept it, Allegra shook her head from side to side. "He hasn't left us, lad. He just…needs help coming back."

"You're the healer. Why can't you save him?"

"I want to. But I can't do this alone. If only…" She looked up at the sound of a great rush of wind that whipped the field of heather, leaving the blossoms swaying about wildly. Two women, wearing flowing gowns of spun gold, appeared beside her.

"Oh, Mum. Gram." Allegra was alternately weeping and laughing as she fell into their arms and embraced them. "I feared you wouldn't come."

"How could we not? Though it has taken us so very long, there is neither distance nor time that could ever separate us from those loved ones who need our help." Her mother's voice was as soft as a lullaby. "Your heart is heavy, my darling."

"Aye, Mum. It's Merrick."

Her mother knelt beside the still body. "This is the man who stole you from our Mystical Kingdom, and carried you away to his?"

"Aye. His name is Merrick MacAndrew."

"And now he's gone to the great beyond, and you're free to return home, my darling."

"Nay, Mum." Allegra dropped to her knees beside her mother. "I'll never be free of Merrick MacAndrew, for I'll carry him in my heart forever."

"In your heart?" Her mother's head came up sharply.

Allegra nodded. "I love him. If he's truly gone, I wish only to join him in that other world."

Her mother glanced over Allegra's head, to meet the knowing look of her own mother.

On a sigh she said, "So. That is how it is." She studied her daughter a moment, then said briskly, "There's no time to waste. We must take him to the Mystical Kingdom, where our power will be greater when joined with that of your sisters."

"Why didn't they come?" Allegra turned to her grandmother.

"Their winged steeds couldn't leave the safety of our kingdom. And we were in too great a hurry to transport them with us. But have no fear. We'll soon join them. Come. We must all gather round the circle if we're to bear Merrick MacAndrew to our home." She cast a glance at the little boy. "Is the lad blood of this man?"

"Aye. This is Merrick's son, Hamish."

Nola took the lad's hand. "Then your strength is truly powerful, Hamish, for the blood that flows from generation to generation is an unbreakable bond. You must come with us. But be warned. What we do in our kingdom will drain us of all power. It could even cost us our lives. Are you willing to pay the price?"

The boy nodded. "I love my father more than anything in this world. Even my own life."

Nola squeezed his hand. "Well said, lad. Come. Join with us."

She waited until all had linked hands. Then she whispered, "I call on the power of the ancient lore. Guide us through the heavens to our own safe shore."

With hands joined, they rose from the ground in a circle with Merrick in the middle. Past flocks of birds they flew. Over mountain peaks they drifted. High over clouds they floated, looking down at the green land below, dotted with villages and flocks and herds. And finally, light as downy feathers, they settled in a verdant meadow, much like the one they'd left behind in Berkshire. But this one was perfumed with the most exotic fragrances. And in the trees flitted tiny fairies, their bodies surrounded by a halo of lights, their musical voices as soft as the tinkling of bells.

"Allegra. Oh, Allegra." Two young women came rushing into Allegra's arms. "You're home at last."

When they moved apart, Allegra turned to Hamish. "These are my sisters, Kylia and Gwenellen."

He could only stare at these two who, though beautiful, looked so different from Allegra. Kylia had hair the color of a raven's wing, plaited into one long fat braid that fell below her waist, and eyes that would rival the heather, ringed with thick, dark lashes. Gwenellen was tiny and fair, with golden tresses that swept almost to the ground, like a veil. Her blue eyes danced in the animated face of a pixie.

"There's no time to waste," Nola told them. "If we're to save the life of this man, we must gather our strengths and share them with him."

"Is this what you desire, Allegra?" Kylia asked.

"Aye. More than anything in this world."

Kylia and Gwenellen shared a quick, startled look before their mother said softly, "Allegra has lost her heart to this man."

"You...love him?" Gwenellen couldn't seem to take it in.

"Aye." Allegra's voice was little more than a choked whisper.

"Then we must help." Kylia quickly grasped her sisters' hands.

"Come, Hamish," Nola called. "For the love you share with your father will be the strongest gift of all."

Catching his hand, she drew him into the circle. The women closed their eyes and began chanting in an ancient tongue. Hamish watched them a moment before closing his own eyes. The chant seemed oddly familiar. He recognized the words as those he'd heard while in a deep sleep. Soon he joined in, lending his voice to theirs.

Time seemed to stop. They might have been there for hours, or mere minutes, while the day turned to dusk, and then to midnight, before dawn light etched the clouds. Birds awoke and sang, joining their voices to the chorus. And then it was once again afternoon, with the sky a clear, cloudless blue.

Suddenly the chanting ended and those in the circle opened their eyes, feeling drained and weary beyond belief. As the others gathered around Merrick, Allegra dropped to her knees beside him and touched her fingertips lightly to his temples.

With her gaze fixed on him she said, "All your wounds are healed now, my love. Wake and come back to us."

Hamish dropped to his knees beside her, watching the fluttering movement behind his father's closed lids. When the lids opened, Merrick's first glimpse of life was the woman looking down at him. There were tears in her eyes, though she was smiling through them. Then he glanced at the lad beside her. Such a handsome lad, with fair hair and gentle blue eyes, whose image had been imprinted forever on his heart.

"Allegra. Hamish." His voice was as rough as though he hadn't spoken in a hundred years. "I thought I'd died." He touched a hand to his chest, but there was no wound, nor even a trace of pain.

"My shoulder..." There, too, he felt for the gaping hole, only to find smooth, unblemished skin.

Understanding came slowly. And then he smiled as he reached a hand to her cheek. "My wonderful, beautiful healer. This was your doing."

She shook her head. "It took all my family's power, plus that of Hamish."

He reached a hand to the lad's. "Even you, my son? Don't tell me you've become a healer now?"

"Aye, Father. Allegra's mother said they needed my love."

Love. Such a miraculous word.

Merrick looked over his son's head to the circle of women around him. "This is your family, Allegra?"

"My mother, Nola." The woman who knelt beside her looked amazingly like Allegra.

"My grandmother, Wilona." She was equally beautiful, with long silver hair.

Allegra's smile grew. "And my sisters, Kylia and Gwenellen."

Merrick sat up, amazed that there was no pain. "How can I thank you for this gift you've given me?"

Wilona spoke for all of them. "We ask no payment. The gifts we've been given must be used only for good, and never for evil. We do ask that you spend the life that's been returned to you in doing only good works.''

He gave a solemn nod of his head. ''That I can surely promise.''

''Now you will desire some food.'' Nola turned toward the cottage in the distance. Then as an afterthought she said, ''Perhaps the lad would enjoy riding one of our winged horses while he awaits his meal.''

The pixie Gwenellen lifted her fingers to her mouth and gave a whistle. Minutes later Hamish's eyes grew round as saucers at the sight that greeted him. A winged horse, pure white, came flying across the sky and landed in the tall grass of the meadow, mere inches away.

''Come, Hamish. I'd like you to meet my steed, Starlight.''

Under Gwenellen's direction the boy lifted a hand and petted the animal's soft muzzle.

''Would you like to ride him?''

Hamish looked over at his father. ''Oh, please, may I?''

Seeing his father's look of concern, Gwenellen said softly, ''There's no reason to fear. I'll ride with the lad and keep him from harm.''

Merrick nodded his approval.

The golden-haired lass lifted the boy to the saddle, then pulled herself up behind him. At her whispered command the horse unfolded its wings and rose into the air.

"Look, Father." With a shout of absolute joy, Hamish waved, then gave a delighted laugh as the horse soared higher and higher, circling overhead.

Merrick got to his feet, shielding the sunlight from his eyes as he watched his son. "He's lost his fear."

"Aye. You would have been proud of him. He had the courage of a warrior when he faced your evil cousins." Allegra stood beside him. "How do you feel?"

He shook his head in disbelief. "Stronger, healthier than I can ever recall. What magic you and your family possess, Allegra."

"Aye. It's potent, my lord. Even stronger than I had realized." She glanced up. "Isn't it grand to hear Hamish laughing?"

He nodded. "There was a time I feared I might never hear the sound of his voice again. Or see his face." He turned to frame her face with his hands. "Or yours, my lady."

Standing a little behind them, Wilona caught Kylia's hand. "I believe we ought to give your mother a hand with the food."

Her granddaughter held back. "I want to stay. I don't remember ever seeing a man before. Nor a man-child. They seem so...different from us and from Jeremy.''

''Aye. They are,'' her grandmother said dryly. ''They're not at all what we've become accustomed to here in our Mystical Kingdom. Now come. We'll allow your sister a moment alone with this stranger.''

''But I want to watch them. I want to see what it is that men and women in love do.''

''Another time.'' With a lilt of laughter Wilona dragged her reluctant young granddaughter toward the cottage.

When they were alone, Merrick touched a hand to Allegra's cheek. ''You look pale, my love.''

''Aye. Mum will prepare food that will give us back the strength we lost while tending you. And then we'll sleep, for rest is healing.''

He framed her face with his hands and stared down into her eyes. ''How can I ever repay you, Allegra? First you gave me back my son, and now you've given me back my life.''

''It wouldn't have been possible if you hadn't been a good and noble man, Merrick. For the chance you've been given is a gift very few receive in this lifetime. It is given only to those deserving.''

At a shout from overhead, they looked up to see the winged horse circling for a landing. When at last Hamish had been helped from its back, he raced across the meadow and flung himself into his father's arms.

"Did you see? Wasn't it grand?"

"Aye. I did see. And I'm envious, for it's something I'll never get to experience, lad."

Hamish turned to Allegra, whose pallor was now more pronounced. "Do you think I could ride Starlight again later?"

"I don't see why not." She leaned heavily on Merrick's arm. "But for now, I must return to my mother's cottage and rest."

Before she'd taken a step Merrick swung her into his arms. Despite her protest, he carried her across the meadow, with Hamish running alongside.

As he drew near the cottage, he was aware of the way her family watched. "Allegra needs to rest."

"Aye." Nola stepped aside. "Her pallet is in there."

He carried her to a small, cozy room and laid her down on the soft pallet. As he straightened, Allegra caught his hand in hers. "Promise me you'll be here when I awake?"

He nodded. "I give you my word."

She was asleep before he stepped from the room.

"You're quiet, Merrick MacAndrew." Nola stepped from the cottage to find Merrick watching as Kylia and Gwenellen frolicked in the meadow with Hamish.

The two young women had fashioned a crown of heather blossoms and placed it on his head before engaging him in a game of hide and seek. The lad's laughter rippled on the breeze, warming Merrick's heart.

He turned. "I was just thinking."

"What about?"

He seemed to collect his thoughts before saying, "It's so peaceful here."

"Aye. It is that."

"You have paradise here in the Mystical Kingdom. No hunger. No evil."

"Some would call that paradise."

"Some?" He glanced at her in surprise. "You don't?"

"Don't misunderstand. As you said, there is much to savor about our kingdom. But it can get lonely at times. And I worry what will happen to my daughters when my mother and I must leave them."

He arched a brow. "You'll die some day? I thought…"

"You thought that because we can save others, we could live forever?" She gave him a gentle smile. "Life and death are but some of the things we all share. The greatest of these is love." She chose her words carefully. "My daughter has given her heart to you, Merrick. I hope you understand the enormity of her gift.''

''I do understand. But in order to be worthy, I must also be willing to sacrifice my own happiness for hers.''

As he stared moodily into the distance, Nola turned and made her way back to the cottage, leaving him alone with his thoughts.

After a rest that might have lasted days or mere hours, they shared a meal. A stew rich with fish from the Enchanted Loch and thick with vegetables from Allegra's garden. Bread still hot from the oven, slathered with freshly churned butter. Mulled wine, to put the bloom back on their cheeks. Tea, dark and strong, to clear the mind. And scones, drizzled with honey, just to satisfy their hearts.

When he'd eaten his fill, Merrick sat back and gave a shake of his head. ''I've traveled the length of this land, from Edinburgh to the Highlands, and I've never tasted a finer meal.''

Nola smiled in acknowledgment of this high compliment. ''Perhaps it's more the company than the food.''

''Aye. The company is fine indeed.'' He glanced around the table at the array of beautiful women, more colorful than a garden of lovely flowers. ''I see now why you find such comfort in this lovely land. It's unlike anything I've ever seen before. There is no knowledge of the passing of time. No discord.''

Wilona sipped her tea. "Perhaps you'd like to stay, Merrick MacAndrew. We've plenty of room for you and your son.''

"If only I could." He glanced at Hamish, who shot him a pleading look. "But I have a duty to my people. They look to me to keep them safe from the ravages of invaders. Without me they would soon see their flocks diminished, their cottages burned, their loved ones harmed and eventually their very lives enslaved.''

"It's never easy putting duty above pleasure.'' Nola glanced at Allegra, who had been very quiet during their meal. Even though her rest had restored her strength, her cheeks seemed unusually pale. "Will you at least stay another night, Merrick?''

He shook his head and pushed away from the table. "I have no idea how much time has passed since we left Berkshire. Days. Weeks. My people will be alarmed. They deserve to learn the truth about my black-hearted cousins, who slew their own neighbors under the guise of barbarians.''

Nola stood, as well. "There is evil in your world, Merrick.'' She saw him glance at Allegra with a thoughtful look. "It is something we'd almost forgotten here in the Mystical Kingdom.''

He nodded. "Unfortunately, it is something I can never forget. I've been forced to spend a lifetime watching for it, fighting against it." His voice lowered with feeling. "There may come a day when good will triumph over evil for all time. But until that day, I must remain vigilant and go on battling it with all the strength I possess."

Nola placed her hand on his. "My daughter was right to fight for your life, Merrick MacAndrew. Yours is a noble calling."

He shook his head in denial. "I'm a warrior, my lady, who has taken many lives on the field of battle. I'm unworthy of your admiration." He held out a hand to his son. "And now Hamish and I must take our leave, if you'll be good enough to lend us a steed."

"You have no need of a horse, Merrick." Nola led the way from the cottage. "My mother and I will use our power to return you and your son to your land."

The others left the table and followed after him.

It was Wilona who noticed Allegra trailing behind with a look of sadness. She paused until her granddaughter caught up with her. "Why this look, my child? The man you love is now healed, and will soon be returned to his people. Is this not what you wanted?"

"Aye." Allegra struggled with tears that threatened. "But I'd hoped that he would return my love enough to take me with him." She glanced at the broad-shouldered man who strode purposefully toward the high meadow, his son by his side.

"Perhaps," her grandmother said softly, "he loves you too much to ask you to go."

"I don't understand."

The old woman merely draped an arm around her granddaughter's shoulders and continued trailing the others.

When they reached the high meadow, the women gathered around Merrick and his son.

Nola joined the boy's hand to his father's and stepped back. "When we form a circle around you, and join our thoughts to yours, you will be returned to your home. You mustn't break contact with each other until you are safely back where you started, or you'll find yourselves right back here in this meadow. Is that understood?"

Merrick nodded, then caught a glimpse of Allegra's face. So pale. So sad. The knowledge that he was the one to cause this pain cut like a knife. But he had to remain strong, for he knew he was doing the right thing. The noble thing. He had no right to take her from all this. She'd already suffered enough for his sake.

He took a step closer, careful not to touch her.

For if he were to touch her now, he'd never have the strength to let go.

Knowing the others were watching and listening, he kept his voice devoid of the passion that burned inside. ''Your mother asked only that I spend the rest of my life doing good. Let it begin with this moment. I love you more than life itself. But this is where you belong, Allegra. Here, where you can be free of the cruelties of my world.''

''Have I nothing to say about this?''

He shook his head, afraid that if he spoke to her again he'd surely fail this, his first test.

He pulled his gaze away from her and nodded to her mother. ''My heart is filled to overflowing with gratitude for the gifts my son and I have been given. And now we bid you farewell.''

Nola chanted the words. ''Leave us then, as you must. Walk always with faith, hope and trust.''

Allegra stood between her sisters and watched as Merrick and Hamish began to rise slowly from the ground. High they soared, then higher still, until they were mere specks on the horizon.

She blinked back tears and watched until they were out of sight. And then, because she couldn't bear to be around the others, she started running and continued until she'd crossed the meadow, seeking out the solitude of her garden, where she would be condemned to a life of loneliness for all time.

Chapter Twenty

Allegra stabbed viciously with her hoe at a weed until it was dislodged. Then she moved on to the next and the next, until her hands ached from the effort.

Hadn't she known her heart could be broken? Hadn't her mother warned her about the cruelties of Merrick's world? What a fool she must have seemed. Throwing herself at him shamelessly. Demanding that he take her. Not just her body, but her heart and soul, as well.

Now he'd gone. And he'd taken part of her with him.

This was worse than any physical pain. That was something she knew how to heal. But this ache around her heart was a festering wound that would never heal. And she had been the one to foolishly invite it.

She'd hoped, but had never really believed, that he might turn his back on his world and stay here in hers. It would be so good for him to be here. To be free of the wars, the cruelties that plagued him. She could admire his reasons for returning to his home. What she couldn't understand was his reason for leaving her behind.

All that talk about being good and noble hadn't lessened the pain of rejection. She stabbed at another weed and tossed it into the growing pile. Maybe he'd thought to spare her, but all he'd done was make it worse.

She heard a sound, like a child's laughter, and lifted her head to peer at Gwenellen's winged horse, Starlight, soaring high above. Puzzled, she lifted a hand to shield the sunlight from her eyes. Were there two figures on the steed's back?

"It isn't a shadow you're seeing, my love. It's Hamish."

At the sound of that deep voice Allegra whirled, to find Merrick standing behind her.

He stood perfectly still, drinking in the sight of her. "He begged for another ride, and your sister was kind enough to accompany him."

"I thought you…" She tried again. "I saw you depart. How did you…?"

He flexed his hand. "My fault. Your mother warned me that Hamish and I would have to link hands until we were home, or we'd end up back here.''

"A mistake?"

"Nay. It was deliberate, I fear." He took a step closer, staring into those sad green eyes. "I've failed my first test."

"Test?"

"Of nobility. I wanted to leave you here, Allegra, where you'd be safe from all evil. I know it was the right thing to do, but I found I couldn't."

"You couldn't?" She was babbling, she knew, but she couldn't seem to stop herself.

He shook his head. "I know I can't stay here, even though it's paradise. My people need me. But if I could persuade you to go with me, as my wife, I'd do everything in my power to make Berkshire as close to paradise as possible."

"Your wife? You wish us to wed, Merrick?"

"More than anything. If you'll have me." As she opened her mouth he lifted a hand. "But I warn you, Allegra, I'll often be away fighting invaders, leaving you alone with a castle to see to, and servants who won't always do things as you wish. When I return I'll be bloody and weary, not fit for such as you. But I give you my word that I'll fight with my last breath to keep you safe, my love. And if we're blessed with children, I'll raise them up to be good and noble, and to honor their mother above all else.

If you agree to leave your home and embrace mine, I promise to love you, Allegra, only you, and cherish you for all the days of my life.''

"Oh, Merrick." She dropped the hoe and crossed the space between them, wrapping her arms around his waist, pressing her mouth to his. "It's all I've ever wanted. More than I could have ever dreamed of."

"Truly? You'd leave all this for me, Allegra?"

At her nod he drew her close and kissed her long and slow and deep. Against her lips he whispered, "Your unselfish love humbles me, Allegra. Now I know I've truly been given back my life."

Merrick stood in the field of heather, his son beside him, watching as the cluster of women, dressed in gowns of jeweled colors, made their way from the cottage. In their midst was Allegra, in a gown of delicate white lace that could have been spun by angels. Her fiery hair hung down her back in a riot of curls that were fastened here and there with sprigs of wildflowers.

The others were chanting as they approached. Ancient words that resembled a hymn of joy. Merrick didn't hear. The women were smiling, though there were tears in their eyes. Merrick didn't see. He was deaf and blind to all but the woman who owned his heart. He had never believed such a woman existed. But here she was, reaching out her hands to his.

As he took them he noted the blisters from the hoe and gave her a heart-stopping smile. "What's this, my little healer?"

She glanced at the blisters. "I was too busy to notice." She closed her eyes a moment, then opened them to find him staring in surprise, for the blisters had disappeared, leaving her flesh as smooth and soft as a newborn's.

"You never cease to amaze me, Allegra."

She smiled. "May it be ever thus, my love."

Love. The word did such strange things to his heart.

Wilona stepped forward, catching their joined hands in hers, and stared into the eyes of this man, who had come to their shores as a threatening stranger and would now become one of them. "There are many gifts that are given to us."

Kylia's voice joined in. "The gift of prophecy. Seeing the past. Foretelling the future."

Nola's voice chimed in. "The gift of healing. Not only the body, but the heart and mind and soul."

Wilona nodded. "But the greatest gift of all is love. Its power is greater than all others. For love can forgive the past, and make clear the future. Love can speak, better than words, to the heart of the beloved. And love can heal. Not only the heart, but the mind and soul, as well.''

She placed her hand on their bowed heads. ''And now, this day, you give your love to one another. In so doing, you are bound for all time. If you are blessed, you will live to see your children's children. And when this life is over, your love will continue through eternity.''

She took a step back. ''Take your son in your arms, Merrick, and join your hand with Allegra's, and we will send you back to your home. We ask only that you return often. For you now have two homes. You and yours will, for all time, call the Mystical Kingdom your home. We are your family. Your people ours. And the gifts we've been given will pass on to you and yours, as well.''

Merrick lifted Hamish in his arms and closed his hand around Allegra's. As her family began to chant, he watched the ground seem to drop away as, ever so slowly, they drifted heavenward.

As they floated over mountaintops and caught glimpses of tiny villages below, he drew his wife close for another lingering kiss. Against her lips he whispered, ''I love you, my wonderful little witch. And will, for a lifetime and beyond.''

Allegra was too overcome to speak. This all seemed like some wonderful, magical dream. This man, who had come to her in anger, was now her noble hero. But he was real. As was the love she felt in her heart.

Love.

It truly was the greatest gift of all. Pure magic. And she would cherish it, and this man, for all time.

* * * * *

In August 2003 be sure to read
THE BETRAYAL,
the second story in Ruth Langan's
enchanting MYSTICAL HIGHLANDS *series!*

Turn the page for a sneak preview!

Prologue

Mystical Kingdom—1547

"Allegra. Gwenellen." Six-year-old Kylia Drummond raced to the edge of the Enchanted Loch, shouting to her sisters over her shoulder. "Come swim with me." Without waiting for them to catch up she began stripping off her gown. Wearing only her chemise, she stepped into the water. When it reached her shoulders she pushed off and began swimming.

She'd always loved the water. Like a lover it called to her. Though there were all manner of deadly creatures in the Enchanted Loch, she had no fear, for such creatures were friendly to her and her family. It was only strangers who needed to beware. The dragon that guarded its shores, and the other monsters that dwelled in the deep, were fiercely loyal to the ones who lived in peace with them here in the Mystical Kingdom.

Seven-year-old Allegra and four-year-old Gwen-ellen took their time stripping off their gowns and stepping gingerly into the frigid water. With squeals of delight they slowly made their way to where Kylia was treading water.

Kylia was holding a piece of netting her mother had fashioned. She paused when she saw sunlight glance off a school of fish that darted by. Moving quickly, she scooped up one from their midst and watched as the school changed direction, the fish quickly disappearing with a flash of light. "I promised Gram I'd bring her some fish for out supper."

"I'll help." Allegra peered into the depths of the clear water. Moving with lightning speed, she caught a fish and deposited it alongside her sister's catch on the shore.

"My turn," Gwenellen cried. She chased several schools, always coming up empty. In desperation she tried one of the spells she'd been learning. But instead of a fish, she found herself holding a dish, which had her sisters giggling. Her smile soon turned into a little pout.

"It doesn't matter." Kylia was quick to soothe her little sister. "We'll have more than enough to fill Gram's pot before we're..." As her words trailed off, she stared into the water with a look of surprise.

"What is it?" Allegra hurried to her sister's side.

"Here." Kylia pointed. "That face. Do you see it?"

Though Allegra and Gwenellen followed her direction, they both shook their heads.

"I see water. Fish. Some rocks far below." Allegra looked up with a frown. "What do you see, Kylia?"

"A man's face. Here." She dipped her hand into the water, then withdrew it hastily when she touched something soft and warm. Human form and flesh shimmering just beneath the waves. "Can you not see?"

When she caught sight of the puzzled looks on her sisters' faces, her tone lowered. "So, he's here for my eyes alone." She accepted her unique gift with the same characteristic matter-of-fact nature that the others accepted theirs. "No matter. I see him clearly. His hair is dark and long, to his shoulders, and his eyes gray and unfathomable. His nose is straight, his chin firm, with a little cleft in it." She sighed as she studied the image. "There's a sadness about him."

"Why is he sad?" Gwenellen asked in hushed tones.

"I know not. But his heart is heavy." Kylia

skimmed her fingers over the ripples of water, then drew back abruptly at the tingle that raced along her arm. "But this I know." She watched as the image shimmered, then dissolved until there was nothing left but rippling water. "One day he and I will meet. And I will learn all the secrets of his heart."

* * * * *

*Will Kylia meet her fantasy man?
Find out in August 2003!*
THE BETRAYAL
Harlequin Historical 670

RUTH LANGAN

traces her ancestry to Scotland and Ireland. It is no surprise, then, that she feels a kinship with the characters in her historical novels.

Married to her childhood sweetheart, she has raised five children and lives in Michigan, the state where she was born and raised. Ruth loves to hear from readers and can be reached by e-mail at ryanlangan@aol.com or on her Web site at www.ryanlangan.com.

Can't get enough of
our riveting Regencies
and evocative Victorians?
Then check out these enchanting
tales from Harlequin Historicals®

On sale May 2003

BEAUTY AND THE BARON by Deborah Hale

Will a former ugly duckling and an embittered
Waterloo war hero defy the odds in the name of love?

SCOUNDREL'S DAUGHTER by Margo Maguire

A feisty beauty encounters a ruggedly handsome
archaeologist who is intent on whisking her away
on the adventure of a lifetime!

On sale June 2003

THE NOTORIOUS MARRIAGE by Nicola Cornick
(sequel to LADY ALLERTON'S WAGER)

Eleanor Trevithick's hasty marriage to Kit Mostyn
is scandalous in itself. But then her husband
mysteriously disappears the next day....

SAVING SARAH by Gail Ranstrom

Can a jaded hero accused of treason and a
privileged lady hiding a dark secret save
each other—and discover everlasting love?

Visit us at www.eHarlequin.com

HARLEQUIN HISTORICALS®

HHMED30

eHARLEQUIN.com

Sit back, relax and enhance your romance with our great magazine reading!

- **Sex and Romance!** Like your romance *hot?* Then you'll *love* the sensual reading in this area.

- **Quizzes!** Curious about your lovestyle? His commitment to you? Get the answers here!

- **Romantic Guides and Features!** Unravel the mysteries of love with informative articles and advice!

- **Fun Games!** Play to your heart's content....

Plus...romantic recipes, top ten lists, Lovescopes...and more!

Enjoy our online magazine today— visit www.eHarlequin.com!

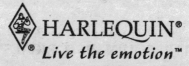

COMING NEXT MONTH FROM

HARLEQUIN HISTORICALS®

BEAUTY AND THE BARON
by **Deborah Hale,** author of LADY LYTE'S LITTLE SECRET
Lucius, Lord Daventry retreated from society after being disfigured in the war. But in order to satisfy his grandfather's dying wish, Lucius proposes a temporary engagement to Angela Lacewood, with the understanding that she'll break it once his grandfather dies. When the old man rallies, will their engagement become a reality?
HH #655 ISBN# 29255-4 $5.25 U.S./$6.25 CAN.

• SCOUNDREL'S DAUGHTER
by **Margo Maguire,** author of NORWYCK'S LADY
When prim and proper Dorothea Bright comes home to reconcile with her estranged father, he is nowhere to be found. Instead, she encounters Jack Temple, a handsome archaeologist who is intent on dragging her along for the adventure—and love—of her life!
HH #656 ISBN# 29256-2 $5.25 U.S./$6.25 CAN.

• WYOMING WIDOW
by **Elizabeth Lane,** author of NAVAJO SUNRISE
Desperate, widowed Cassandra Riley Logan claims that the missing son of a wealthy Wyoming rancher is the father of her unborn child. His family takes her in, and Cassandra finds herself drawn to Morgan, the missing man's brother. But when her secret threatens to tear them apart, will their love be strong enough to overcome Cassandra's reluctant deception?
HH #657 ISBN# 29257-0 $5.25 U.S./$6.25 CAN.

• THE OTHER BRIDE
by **Lisa Bingham,** Harlequin Historical debut
Though Lady Louisa Haversham is married by proxy to a wealthy American, she isn't ready to settle down. Instead, she convinces her maid, Phoebe Gray, to trade places with her. As Phoebe, Louisa must now masquerade as a mail-order bride. Gabe Cutter, the trail boss escorting several mail-order brides to their grooms, proves to be a thorn in her side—and a constant temptation!
HH #658 ISBN# 29258-9 $5.25 U.S./$6.25 CAN.

KEEP AN EYE OUT FOR ALL FOUR OF THESE TERRIFIC NEW TITLES

HHCNM0403